Frederick William Wyon

**Edwin and Ethelburga**

A drama

Frederick William Wyon

**Edwin and Ethelburga**
*A drama*

ISBN/EAN: 9783337304584

Printed in Europe, USA, Canada, Australia, Japan

Cover: Foto ©Andreas Hilbeck / pixelio.de

More available books at **www.hansebooks.com**

# EDWIN AND ETHELBURGA,

## A Drama.

BY

## FREDERICK Wᴹ WYON.

LONDON:

SMITH, ELDER AND CO., 65, CORNHILL.

———

M.DCCC.LX.

# PERSONS REPRESENTED.

———✦———

OSRIC, an old Danish lord.

ESMUND, his Esquire.

EDWIN, a young Saxon lord, whose father had been formerly
dispossessed of his castle by Lord Osric.

HOSKOLD, a crafty Dane, and a retainer of Lord Osric.

ERIC, an old retainer of Lord Osric.

THEODORE, a Greek boy, affectionately attached to Lord Edwin.

OSWITH,
HUBERT, } Retainers of Lord Edwin.

ETHELBURGA, daughter of Lord Osric.

Various minor characters.


SCENE, either in a forest, or in Lord Osric's castle ; once in a
village.

# PROLOGUE.

Now in the centre of the mystic stage

I stand, a god, my spirits at command,

To bring a world upon 't for two brief hours.

Fade, Earth! come, bliss of Heav'n, and thoughts more

      bright

Than the worn mould of this dull life provide!

And thou too, Sorrow, give me leave awhile;

Lay not thy heavy and all-quenching hand

On the swift spirit of invention.—

Honour, step forth! thou scarce remember'd dame,

Sneer'd from the world by low-brow'd hypocrites,

E'en with that eye of Juno come, when thou

Didst rock the cradle of young Albion !

Go, seek old Osric's breast; shine in him, touch

The frosts of eighty winters with thy glow.

Next thou, Nobility, set thy true stamp

Upon young Edwin, that he be adorn'd

With ev'ry grace that fits a gentleman,

And worthy subject of an empress' love.

Fly, Virtue, to sweet Ethelburga's heart !

There shalt thou find a beauteous temple rare,

Which thou, O goddess, shield (for well thou canst)

From the lewd fire of assailing eyes.

Passion ! thou shalt have licence large to-day :

Esmund thy quarry, whom griev'd Nature framed

To spread her fame, and in the forefront shine

Of all her kind.    Ill Counsel, to his ear !

Bury in wicked Hoskold thy dark soul.

But, lastly, thou, O spirit, that all survey'st,

All things inform'st with thy sweet subtle fire,

Bright, mystic, glorious, peerless sov'reign Love !

Be present, and inspire each character ;

Grant life and breath to all, and to thy priest

Reprieve from censure and the scorn of men !

# EDWIN AND ETHELBURGA.

---

## ACT I.

### SCENE I.—THE FOREST.

*Enter* EDWIN *and* THEODORE.

*Edw.* Enough, sweet Theodore ; go, play, dear boy ;

I'll hear thy music at a merrier time.

*The.* Why is Lord Edwin sad ?    The live-long day,

With leaden step has he paced to and fro,

Putting the merry forest out of tune.

Why have I seen him oft o'erslouch his brows ?

Then, while to pleasure him, the sweet birds sang

Under their green roofs, mid the summer leaves,

1

In misplaced melancholy sit alone,

And muse, and sigh, and cover up his face

Within his hands, until a tear stole through?

Why is Lord Edwin sad?

*Edw.*                    I cannot tell.

*The.* Say rather, that you will not.

*Edw.*                              Cease to inquire:

I am not sorrowful, if something sad.

Times are, 'tis sweeter to be sad than merry;

Say, this is so.

*The.*        But is it sweet to weep?

Flows pleasure in salt tears?   Or all at once

Does melancholy seize upon the soul

Where never that dark humour dwelt before?

For, till we lately to this forest came,

I never saw you sad.

*Edw.*            Well, well; thou'rt right:

This forest's sight has filled my soul with grief:

There rest thee, Theodore, and ask no more.

Thou canst not aid me with thy little strength

To do the business that I have in hand:

Nor would I stain thy young brow with my cares,

Because I love thee much, dear Theodore.

   *The.* O monstrous love ! to be so double-faced,

To pat my cheek, and wound me at the heart :

All sting, no honey ; like a cruel wasp !

Thou wrong'st me,—oh ! thou dost ; I say, thou dost ;

When, day by day, thy very eyes have seen

My strength grow to the level of my love.

Why dost thou love me, say ?

   *Edw.*               Thou foolish boy !

Who can say why he loves ?   Thyself say how

Thou mak'st thyself belov'd.   Think, if you will,

My heart, debarr'd from other vent, so spends

Its soft and sentimental part on thee.

   *The.* Come, say what's forward.

   *Edw.*             Willingly, I would ;

But that the tale might ruffle thee with fear.

   *The.* In twilight does each tree a ghost appear.

A secret's worst is in the worst way told,

When secrets in friends' faces friends behold :

For mystery sets Fancy on the wing,

To spy a bugbear in each mortal thing ;

Which, if 'twere seen with vision less alarm'd,

Were of its dreadful colours half disarm'd :

As many terrors as the breast appal,

Uncertainty is mother of them all.

*Edw.* Thy love hath conquer'd : come, I'll tell thee all.

Sit closer, Theodore : put by thy lute.

*The.* I'll hang it on this bough, to catch the wind,

That's full of love-sighs.—Oh, the silly wind !

'Twill measure out its sorrows by the hour,

And sometimes die outright of pure despair ;

But the next moment up it springs again,

And screams and raves with fury and mad rage.

*Edw.* This England, as thou know'st, is my birth-land ;

Nor far from this, stands my ancestral right,

A castle hoar, whose high abutting front

Looks forth upon the deep ; here I was born.

Now, when I was a child less old than thou,

A most ferocious, bloody brood of men

Came sudden from the North.    Ere yet was time

To arm resistance, on our gates they pour'd,

Struck down half-rais'd defence, swarm'd in and in,

Rush'd through the chambers like the blast of doom,

And smote, and smote till stone walls rung with shrieks,

And under-whisper'd groans, muffled with blood.

My father,—canst recal him, Theodore ?

 *The.* Dim, through the vision of my childish days,

His aged face breaks sad and sorrowful.

 *Edw.* Oh, he had cause ; for while hard-press'd he
  fought,

My mother, then in second pregnancy,

Flew shrieking to his side ; yet, ere she reach'd him,

He saw her caught by th' hair and instantly

Brain'd by these devils.    In a distant room

I lay asleep, but suddenly I woke

And saw my father bending o'er my crib,

With armour all aflame, and fearful looks.

He caught me out, and strain'd me to his breast:

I hung about his neck, and scream'd for fright.

A blasphemous and blood-besmeared crew

Pursued him close : he laid me quickly down,

Caught up his axe, and sprang into the doorway.

Then I beheld him, (for it was a sight

To print remembrance on an infant's brain,)

Upon the threshold, root his firm left foot ;

His spacious chest unfold, that heav'd with fire :

Aloft he rais'd his arms, and in his eye

Defiance flam'd.

*The.*        Strike with thy soldier, Heaven !

Descend upon thy cause, and show thyself.—

Oh, did he fall ?

*Edw.*        No, boy, he did not fall :

For, as he stood thus firm, confronting Death

Who dark and closely overshadow'd him,

The leader of those men, a noble Dane,

Was fired with sympathy : he offer'd terms ;

And so, to save his child, my father stoop'd

To be a captive.

*The.*          What befell him next ?

*Edw.* To serve the sea-kings : but he grew belov'd

Of these rough spirits ; and of his brother slaves

So valiantly esteem'd, that, on occasion,

They, giving vent to their affections,.

Chose him their leader.

*The.*                    See, how inborn worth

Communicates itself: though overspread

With thickest smoke of fortune, it shines through,

And draws all knees to its confessed light.

*Edw.* For many years we roved the desert seas,

My sire, and I. and fifty valiant men,—

Fresh, jolly, lawless, appetitive hearts,

Chance-fed like the sea-eagles, and o'erroof'd

By blue ethereal Jove.   To do our wills,

In mere blind spirit of obedience,

They would have plunder'd heaven of her stars,

And snatch'd the silver moon from out the sky.

Ha ! ha ! when o'er the horizon peep'd our poles,

To mark the trader droop his fearful sail,

And creep into his hole !   The music faint,

The dancers shrick, coy maidens fly to th'arms

Of their spurn'd youths, who faster fled than they ;

While like a furious and on-striding ghost,

The beacon flamed alarm from hill to hill.

 *The.*  O Lord, the merry life o' the blue sea !

When shall I see 't again ?   Oh, when shall I

Be rock'd upon 't once more ?   Down, down to sink

Into the cavern of the awful deep,

And watch the wat'ry peril hang o'erhead,

Then, take the huge wave at his mighty spring,

And touch the stars ! Anon, with sheet set fair

To the rough toying of the am'rous breeze,

Through the crest-tossing billow-ranks to ride,

Like Phœbus on his cloud-dividing steeds,

The mark of gods and men !   The music, heart !

The music of the hurly-burly sea,

When to our songs he roar'd his boist'rous bass,

And, as our jovial cups we clink'd, would come

Bolt at the vessel's side, and leap aboard !

Ho ! ho ! the fright that stain'd each cheek with death,

Or ever we came near : was not a fish

But thrust his bottle nose ten fathom deep,

And trembled in his cave.

*Edw.* Peace, peace, thou little prating fool ! be still :

But I've a tale to make thee steadier.

Once, being set upon a Moorish barque,

We, in the teeth of a determin'd foe,

Forc'd bloody entrance.   All resistance slain,

Or bound, we search'd the ship ; and in the hold,

Found certain men, in chains ; most mis'rably

Pent up in darkness, filth, and pestilent air.

Among the rest, a pretty, pale Greek boy

Droop'd o'er his dying father.

*The.*                           Thine own hand

Undid the knotty bonds my father bore :

But when his limbs were free, methought I saw

His spirit come into his eyes, and smile ;

Then soar beyond his body, that grew pale

For very envy, that it could not follow.

*Edw.* In fine, for this thou know'st, my father died ;

And those who serv'd him with united voice

Swore to myself obedience.   For awhile

I sway'd these stormy hearts, these leashless wills,

Their head and demigod.   Yet in the breast

Of pleasure, mid all jovial circumstance,

Full oft the solitary thought would spring

That poisons joy.   'Twas for my native land

This sickness, that stole o'er my secret soul

Till it outgrew the use and habit of mirth,

And life wax'd tedious.   Finally I chose

From all my crew some fifty volunteers,

English kin-spirits, to my fortunes link'd,

And with a weary heart forswore the sea.

Now with my little band, yet strong in trust,

And thee, my Theodore, I stand once more

On mine own—homeless.   This same forest, where

Methinks the birds sing nought but dirges now,

Was once my theatre of throng'd delight.

Ah me! how mournful, dull, and leaden-cold,

Through each remember'd glade, the echo sounds
Of my strange manly feet! On this sweet bank,
O'erarch'd with massy leaves, my mother sate,
And watch'd me, as I play'd—Ah, memory!
There's not a tree, in all this wilderness,
But hath a voice, and hoarsely finds it out
To tell the story of departed days.
Upon the forest's verge my castle stands,
And frowns at me from its arm'd battlements.

*The.* Let cunning Fancy not beguile my lord,
Win it, and it shall smile, and turn about
Its armed teeth upon its present friends.
Why, what's a castle but the world in brief,
That dotes upon success and shelters it,
But at misfortune bristles virtuously?

*Edw.* True, boy, thy wit makes thee a senator.
Tickle sad sorrow with a merry jest
Until she smile.   'Tis folly, sure, to sit
With folded arms and sigh.   Hence from my breast,
Vain grief! henceforth I'll feast my thoughts on war.

*The.* What is his name, the lord who holds your
    castle ?

*Edw.* Lord Osric, boy, if he be yet alive.

I have sent to him an ambassador

To crave a battle, that my cause may come

To Heav'n's arbitrament.—Look yonder, boy:

Are they not dress'd like Danes, who come this way ?

Let us stand out of sight.

*Enter* ESMUND *with* HOSKOLD.

*Hos.* Oh, yet in pity hear me ! look, sir squire ;

My guilt's mine own,—all mine : t' expose it, were

To slay the innocence of my wife and babes,

Who with myself will be cast forth to die.

Consider it, sir squire, consider it :

How little is he wrong'd, who, being robb'd,

Can from his plenty not perceive the theft.

Our faults but testify that we are men ;

But he, who shutteth mercy from his breast,

Seems less than human.

*Esm.*                 Canst thou plead so fair,

Damn'd as thou art, in act ?   Ungrateful cur,

That  bit  thy  master's  hand !   Thou  worse  than

    beast :

Thou thing without a conscience, hear thy crime!

Naked, thou camest to our castle gates,

Thou, and thy wife, and shiv'ring little ones :

To pity moved by thy beseeching tale,

Thy tears, thy miseries, thy helplessness,

I drew thee from the cold, and housed thee warm :

I brought thee to my lord, who heard thee kindly ;

And, of his bounty, thou wert clothed and fed :

But when thy soul revived, and thou grew'st strong,

So warm'd the viper in thy guilty breast :

Unholy wretch ! thou didst purloin from him

Who gave thee life.

    *Hos.*                 It hath a golden tongue,

Temptation.

    *Esm.*           Gratitude, a heavenly one.

    *Hos.* My shame and penitence have struck me dumb.

*Esm.* And therefore will I overlook thy guilt :

Restore what thou hast taken, and my tongue

Shall not accuse thee to thy injur'd lord.

*Hos.* Most generous ! Oh, yet a second time

My saviour ! Thou hast touched me to the quick

By mercy. Oh, thou wrong'st the veriest thief

E'er swung on gallows, if thou thought his heart

Incapable of thanks ! This life thou'st saved,

I, from this hour devote to thee; henceforth

No charge of thine shall be so perilous,

Or grown so nigh to the pale edge of death,

But I will risk it for brave Esmund's sake.

Hast thou no present trust for me ?

    *Esm.*                      No, none.

    *Hos.* I'm sorry for it, since my zeal is hot.

Think o'er 't again.

    *Esm.*        Still none ; at least not now.

    *Hos.* More's in thy heart than speaks. Say, art thou
        crossed

In the bright path of thine ambition ?

His name!—and he o'ershadows thee no more:

Or stands some babe betwixt thyself and fortune ?

Him will I steal, and to the forest bear,

To find his nurse among the hungry wolves.

   *Esm.* Irresolution !   Oh, how oft have I       *Aside.*

In thought leagued with this villain : yet, all things

Falling miraculously to my wish,

And opportunity beseeching speech,

My tongue falls dumb.   O virtue ! is't thy voice

That chokes the guilty passage ?

   *Hos.*                    Then, farewell :

I see, thou wilt not trust me.   Half thy tale

Blushes upon thy cheek :  well, well ;  how shame

Steals from a man all but the manly name.

   *Esm.* Fellow, thou growest rude.

   *Hos.*                My zeal did err,

And 'tis my zeal asks pardon.

   *Esm.*                I am harsh ;

Hoskold, forgive it me :  thou may'st be false,

But well thou canst play honesty:  I own,

Thy bluntness hath more oped my bosom, than

A speech of finer point.   Come hither, friend ;

I will confess so much : I am not happy.

   *Hos.* Marry, then use all means thou canst to be so.

   *Esm.* Man, as thou fear'st thy Sovereign above,

Wilt thou be secret of my confidence ?

   *Hos.* Sir Esmund, 'twas my love that swore e'en

      now

To serve thee : what avails to double oaths ?

Keep thine own counsel, if thou wilt mistrust me.

   *Esm.* Then listen, and I will unfold my grief :—

Lord Osric hath a daughter to his age,

Fair Ethelburga, whom I will not praise,

Lest I should slander a celestial saint.

Enough, I love her ; and, in her sweet quest,

Have wearied out a fruitless, misspent youth,

Which, else devoted, might have brought me to

Those shining goals of men, wealth and renown.

For she, or whether o'er my rank she soars,

Or that my person and rude soldier's tongue

Those graces lack that give affection wings,

Disdains the love that I do set on her.

Oft have I moved her, yet no favour won ;

To all entreaty is her heart love-proof ;

Till, when with grief and pain she sees me pale,

Her pity through her cloud of anger breaks,

And looks upon me with that rosy light

Might draw a damnèd spirit back to life.

Thus paradise hangs ever at my lip ;

Still, as I near it, flies ; still lures me on ;

And still my hope-enthralled feet pursue.

*Hos.* The miseries, sighs, lamentations, tears,

Sickness, and pains of heart, and weariness,

Griefs in all attitudes, and without name,

To make description weep to think upon,

That follow in the haggard train of love !

All Neptune hath distilled through lovers' eyes,

And from no other source derived his salt :

Old Boreas, who through the wood howls now,

Blew careless music from his jolly lungs,

Until his breath was tainted with love-sighs.

What man who in his bosom bears a heart,

And hath not proved a woman's subtlety ?

Look, when she smiles, she masks an inward storm :·

But when she would be gracious, oft she frowns.

Let wit be mute in woman's company,

And reason speak in sov'reign manliness.

Oh, sir, 'tis very much to be reproved,

That man, t'whose throne the great Creator link'd

Fair universal nature, should beseech

Favours that are his due : produce the rule,

And woman, in her turn, makes suit to apes,

Apes sue to fishes : yet, bore nature sway,

Woman in man should clearly recognize

Her prophet, priest, and king, and something more.

Look round, and glean experience with thine eye :—

Mark, how the fame of valour, show of strength,

A loud imperious tone, and lofty bearing,

Though wit be scant, draw woman's suffrages ;

Such man is pester'd and pursued by maids,

Till he abhor virginity ; while he,

Who, pale and silent, in the sunshine sits

Of the charm'd circle of his mistress' eye,

Winging his weary heart with true love-sighs,

And nightly nourishing his suit with tears,

For all requital hath his lady's scorn.

   *Esm.* Then, prythee, what wouldst thou enjoin me to ?

   *Hos.* To get her in thy pow'r,—to force thy suit.

   *Esm.* Peace, fellow ! lest thy words, profanely piercing

The sacred stillness of this leafy dell,

May breathe a voice in oaks, to strike thee dumb.

   *Hos.* Why, this it is, to give a saint advice :

Either be all for Heav'n, or not at all.

Take Virtue to thy heart, and shun thy love.

   *Esm.* It is a blessed thing, to sleep in peace.

   *Hos.* Sleep singly then, and envy not the man,

Who to his bosom shall entreat thy love.

   *Esm.* Ah, Hoskold ! there thou wound'st me verily.

Didst thou know how exceedingly I burn,

And am consumed, and tortured in this flame !

In sober truth, I am a man no more ;

Nor have a heart for anything on earth,

Save only to be mis'rable.

  *Hos.*      Be happy.

 *Esm.* Then am I lost.

 *Hos.*      Why, then, be virtuous.

 *Esm.* O God ! despair lies upon that side too.

I live in Hell, to earn my death in Heav'n,

And suffer for a promise, in the trial

And conflict of our souls, that then's most dark :

Ah, gamester, on what desp'rate die thou stak'st !—

Thine heart, thine all, upon a dubious gain !

Heaven ? 'tis in the bosom of my love :

Then Heav'n itself is Hell, if she's not there ;

And Hell with her were Heav'n enough for me.

My mind is toss'd about betwixt two seas ;

Fate, bring me then to anchor, how she please.

  *Hos.* Unhappy man, give o'er ; thou plagu'st thy-

   self :

What, be not thine own devil.   List to me :—

It is thy lady's wont each week to seek

A village, that beyond the forest lies.

   *Esm.* Ay, to o'ersee her father's tenantry.—

Oft have I seen my heart's sweet sovereign,

Encircled with her rustic worshippers,

Hearing their silly suits and grievances ;

Or, with the magic of her bright-beam'd eye,

Healing their quarrels ; e'en her presence hath

A harmony that quells contentious thoughts ;

Or alms-bestowing, with a grace so apt,

The tongue lies mute in the receiver's mouth,

Choked with the heart's commissions.

   *Hos.*                              At day's close,

Through this same forest homeward she returns,

Thyself in company to guard her safe.

Now, here will I, with sundry men of trust,

Lie secretly in ambush ; and, when ye

Approach, rush out, and bear thy mistress off.

On Brackley moor, there stands a ruin'd house ;

Come thither to thy love, and urge thy suit.

*Esm.* Do, as thou wilt; but, prythee, say no more.

*Hos.* I'll to my fellows then : seek thou thy love :

All shall be ready, ere thou com'st with her.        [*Exit.*

*Esm.* Shades of mine ancestors, whose martial deeds

Blazed in the virtuous front of the noonday,

To the eternal shame of secret plots !—

Oh, gloriously enthroned o'er erring men !

Look not upon me now, lest reason sink

Beneath those holy, still, and quenchless fires :

Let me be coverèd with mine own sin,

That Heav'n hold me no more in memory.

Pure-thoughted girl ! angel of innocence !

Two souls eclipse not with thy cruelty !

I would unlock desire with lawful key,

And save thee with a priest's chaste warranty :

But spurn my love, and sue thy friend in Heav'n ;

In me thou'st none : yet to my pray'rs prove kind ;

And I'll requite this wooing of hot youth

With an eternity of wedded truth.        [*Exit.*

*The.* A fox ! a fox ! Lord, wilt thou not give chase ?

*Edw.* Run, Theodore, to Hubert, my chief man ;

And bid him through the forest wind his horn,

To call my men : I'll follow instantly.

*The.* Mark me ; I'm here, and now I'm gone.

[*Exit, running.*

*Edw.* Poor lamb !

The wolf hath come thee villanously near,

And, but thine heav'nly shepherd waked, thou'dst bled.

'Tis true thy father is mine enemy ;

But treachery is a disguised devil,

Who's foe alike to all. I hear my horn

Startle the forest glades with echoing shrill :

I'll go, and with my presence urge despatch. [*Exit.*

———◦◇◦———

## SCENE II.—A VILLAGE.

*Enter* VILLAGERS, MUSICIANS, *&c.*

1*st Vill. (woman).* Now, by thine eye, thou lov'st me.

2*nd Vill. (man).* Sweet, I do.

1*st Vill.* Ah, me ! how grew division 'twixt us
two ?

Say, did the treason through thine eye creep in ?

Or was't my scolding lips first sow'd the sin ?

Sweet love, the quarrel in thine eye began,

That corresponded with bold Marian ;

Though through the village 'tis for ever told,

She's ugly as a witch, and quite as old :

Ye had your signals——

> 2*nd Vill.*                    Dearest, say not this.

> 1*st Vill.* Tell me, she's plain.

> 2*nd Vill.*                    Sweet, if you think,
> she is.

1*st Vill.* Forgive me, then, if I did sulk and pout ;—

Who would not do it, being so put out ?—

And be more loving to me than of late.

> 2*nd Vill.* I'll press my pardon on thy lips, my
> Kate.                    [*They retire.*

> 3*rd Vill.* Since Heav'n was pleased to take away my
> wife,—

Not yet two months,—how barren seems this earth

Of every solace it was wont to have!

Sure none but fools would in this world know

 mirth,

When not a spot each treads on but may be

The laugher's grave.   Ye hills, whose nodding brows

Salute the morn, ye meadows and green vales,

I have no pleasure now to look upon ye,

For ye remind me that I once was happy.   [*He retires.*

 4*th Vill.* I will not be denied to look upon her.

 5*th Vill.* Well, well; I've warn'd thee to keep from

  her sight.

When Master Peter gave account of thee,

I saw her cheek inflame with sudden fire:

Thou'rt ruin'd if she look upon thee now.

Go, hide thee, till thy credit be repair'd.

 4*th Vill.* As moth to flame, or to the magnet,

  steel,

Or this gross earth to the celestial sun,

So am I drawn to her.            [*They retire.*

*Mus.*                Look to your parts ;
My Lady Ethelburga comes this way.


*Enter* ETHELBURGA.


SONG.

Under a stately-tressèd tree,
When quiet eve breathed sweet and holy,
A youth lay,—none so sad as he,
That feed with melancholy ;—
    " My love's forsworn,
    Her vows hath torn ;
    Let me die, and quit life's folly."
*All.* Oh, let me die, and be forgot :
    What is life, where love is not ?


O'er the forest leaves she comes,
Tripping with her little feet ;
On the grass she kneels her down,—
    " Art thou there, my sweet ?
    Do not chide ;
    For beside
    Thine, my heart doth truly beat."
*All.* Welcome, sweet sunny love, sweet April life,
    That lives at death of cold, rough Winter's strife.

All around her steals his arm,
   Tender light breaks through his frown,
On his bosom falls her head
   Gently, gently down.
      Wake, breezes ! flow
     In murmurs soft and low,
And, wrapping round, love's faint sweet spirit drown.
*All.* Hush ! hark ! no sound : the moon sleeps still
In valley, and o'er grass-clothed hill.


*Eth.* How moving is the voice of harmony

In silence breathed, under the fall of eve !

Methinks the night bends an attentive ear

And hither throngs more fast, while the faint stars

Show forth their tim'rous heads, to be resolved

What heav'nly creature 'tis that charms the air.

Friends, sing again, yet not so sadly now,—

A song that trips unto a merry tune.


### SONG.

Who will be a forester,
   And in the greenwood dwell ;
All day to chase the flying deer
.   Through copse and mossy dell ?

A yew-tree bow with arrows keen
    Upon his shoulder rattle ;
The spear gleams in his hand that shall
    Do with the chafed boar battle.

Ho ! holloa ! ho ! the deer bounds past ;
    His dog looks in his face ;—
Away ! away !—from far the blast
    Brings back the furious chase ;—

Till when at eve the western sun
    The em'rald trees doth tan ;
Back to his forest home comes he,
    A toilworn, hungry man.

Where Marian at her rose-twined door,
    In kirtle white dress'd neatly,
Him welcomes to her outspread store,
    And kisses sweetly, sweetly.

Who will be a forester,
    And in the greenwood dwell ?
Who loves with me sweet liberty,
    This life shall suit him well.

*All.* Then hey ! hark, how my horn winds through the hollow !
    All ye who would pleasure, come follow me, follow !

*Eth.* Hath any man beheld Sir Esmund yet ?—

Sweet friends, my heart requites your melody

Beyond report of my untutor'd tongue.

*Mus.* We'll sing again.

*Eth.*                     I pray ye, sing no more.

Lest pleasure surfeit of sweet sounds, and die :

Too oft repeated sweets find wings, and fly.—

But see, the fire of slow-climbing eve

Is brightly kindled in the tall tree-tops,

To all pacific roamers on the wing

The signal for home-flitting.   If I stay

Much farther on the wrong side of this wood,

My fears will make me too a wingèd thing.

O Esmund, thou must needs be changeable

On a sudden, if thou canst be so remiss ;

But late thy fault was much the other way,

I could not rid my garment of thy pray'rs.

O God be thank'd ! he comes.


*Enter* ESMUND.


*Esm.* My love and service to your ladyship !

*Eth.* Thou comest late ; but that my fears forgive,

Because thou com'st at all.

*Esm.*                        What ? angry, lady ?

Oh, chide me with a smile, if thou wilt chide.

*Eth.* Let us set forth.   Who is't, that weeps in black ?

[*To* 3rd *Vill.*

The best of men in tears, my sorrowing Maurice !

How shall I comfort thee ?   Alas, good man !

And yet, alas ! my comfort is so small ;

Death has broke ope thy thrifty store of joy,

And stol'n thy treasure with his greedy hand.

We are all sport of that same cruel fiend :

But think, good Maurice ; think, thou woful man,

How short his triumph, and thine own, how vast,

When, through the dark and speechless vault of death,

The trump of resurrection shall sound ;

And thou, rising from sleep, shalt gaze on Christ,

Where, robed in awful majesty, He stands,

With many legions of bright-mailèd saints,

In the full hour of fated victory !

And when, from rank to rank, from choir to choir,

From height to height of the celestial throng,

The harps of seraphs shall advance his praise,

Till silence shall eschew itself and sing,—

Thou shalt behold, and meet, and to thee clasp

Thy risen, glorious, and transfigur'd wife,

To anchor on thy breast eternally.

Oh, think on this, thou woe-bewilder'd man,

And lift thyself above these clouds of care.

3rd Vill. And so I will, and put my trust in Him,

Unto whose pity I commend my tears.

Eth. Possessing hope, thou still enjoy'st thy lost one.—

Please you, Sir Esmund, that we now proceed.—

Oh, infamous! thou bold notorious man      [To 4th Vill.

That, wanting virtue, hast cast off the cloak

Of vice, mute shame, since thou has dared to meet me

In all the glaring newness of thy guilt.

What, thinkest thou thy character is dumb?

O villain! hath not guilt a tongue of fire

To brand itself in th' eyes of righteous men?

Thine actions, do they not proclaim thee, wretch?

Thy thefts, lusts, slanders, thy false-swearing lips?

Thy beastly and perpetual drunkenness ?

Thy words profane, that ope the wounds of Christ ?

Go, look upon thy fields, which thou neglect'st,

To sow this peaceful village o'er with broils.—

Answer me not, thou God-abandon'd man;

With my reproof shall end thy tenancy :

Here thou abid'st no more.—I am too harsh ;

I see repentance swimming in thine eye,

And honesty, like the rich-laden bark

That o'er its limits swells the rising wave,

Float in upon that tide : I'll pause awhile.—

Farewell to all who love me.

     *Villagers.*            Blessings with you !

     *Esm.* Keep back, keep back, ye rude unmanner'd

     clowns,

Out of my lady's path : ye are too forward.

     *Eth.* O shame, shame, shame ! Sir Esmund, cruel

     man !

Wilt thou scorn love because its nature is

To rush in front of manners ?    Oh, to me

How fairer seems, and more to be desired

The rough, rude spirit of affection,

Though saucy, reckless, wild and turbulent

As th' ocean-foam that beats the doors of Heav'n,

Than thin profession lisp'd in choicest terms.—

Farewell again to all.                    [*Exeunt.*

## SCENE III.—THE FOREST.

*Enter* HOSKOLD *and another.*

*Hos.* What humours are in men! say, shall I laugh?

Or should it rather be a cause for tears,

To mark the ways of mad capricious love?

The dull grow witty, but the wise turn fools:

Those that were joyous once as summer flies,

Are mopers now to think upon their love,

Detest the world, forswear its company

But to be closeted with their sweet thoughts:

Yet see the man, t'whom not his bosom friend

Gave credit for the wealth of ten poor words,

As swift as fire talk down an orator

That would calumniate his mistress' chin.

I, the philosopher, am most the fool,

Because I love a man, who is in love,

And follow him as he his love pursues

For the reward of one approving look.

Yea, though the world beside accounts me villain,

Nor wrongs me much, for gallant Esmund's sake

Would I heap more damnation on my soul.

To see a man of noble qualities,

In counsels wise, in execution swift,

Brave, generous, of an exalted mind,

Grovel his greatness at a vain girl's feet

Who loves him not!   What maiden ever did

Requite the man who loved her most of all ?

I cannot teach my Esmund how to lisp

Or sing love's praises to the liquid lyre,

But I will show a royal road to woo.

The end of love is surely to win love,—

What matters then how won, if only won ?

Whether 'tis conquered or persuaded fair ?

Maids look not at the means when they're undone.—

Say, fellow, art thou perfect in thy part ?

Thou art ?   Stand back, then, till I signal thee.

*They retire.*


*Enter* ESMUND *and* ETHELBURGA.

*Esm.* Chide me no further, lady : a reproof

From those we love is as a volume spoken.

Like a stern wind around a ruin'd house,

Thou but reprov'st a heart that's desolate,

And empty of all joy.

*Eth.*                I'll say no more,

Unless it be with words to unsay my words,

And heal thee with that weapon caused thy wound.

I was too swift to judge a swift rash tongue :

Forgive me, if I grieved thee ; but thou didst—

Grant it, thou didst offend me grievously.

*Esm.* Jesu ! am I not mortal ? who could see,

That from his heart look'd forth, these ragged clowns

3—2

Cheering their faces in thy sun-bright eye,

And feel no envy ?

    *Eth.*               Thou dost grow too warm.

    *Esm.* My heart's on fire, and shall my tongue be cool ?

Hast thou or heart to feel or eye to judge,

And rat'st me less in passion than the Finn

Whose spirit's bound in ice ?  I love thee, lady;

Yet have more strength than skill to tell thee so.

Oh, by whatever name shall I conjure thee ?

(For well thy beauty graces every name,)

My joy ! my grief ! my death ! my life ! my bane !

Why shunn'st thou Esmund, who would die for thee ?

Alas ! my person hath no shape of love ;

Nor is my tongue endued with happy skill

To tinkle sweetly in a lady's ear,

Yet this my merit,—that I love thee, lady.

When other men shall paint thee with their praise,

Count thy perfections with a ready tongue,

And I alone sit silent, cold and still,

This be my merit and redeeming grace,

That I adore thee more than all beside.

For loudest speakers but commend themselves,

Their heart still echoes back the flattery

Which they would heap on others : but true love,

When he would move a soul in trees or rocks

With the swift fire of his conscious speech,

Summons his spirits quickly to command,

Then like a vaunting general grows pale,

Falters, and dies in his own eloquence.

Be moved then, Ethelburga, with my suit,

At least for charity, and scorn not love,

Lest thou hereafter of scorn'd love be scorn'd.

   *Eth.* Enough, no more : cease, and for ever cease.

Have I not told thee twenty thousand times,

I will not hear thy suit ?   I love thee not.

   *Esm.* Thy reason, lady ?   Oh, declare my fault !

   *Eth.* I have none other than a lady's reason ;

I love thee not, because I do not love thee,

Nor would a gentle mind solicit more.

Till late, I held thee in my best esteem ;

My sire,—nay I, and all—stand in thy debt,

For thou art valiant, active, skill'd and wise,

And gifted with the eye and spirit of rule,

By which, thou hast reform'd our warriors,—

A service beyond thanks in these fierce times,

When death flies o'er the sea on ev'ry wind.

To these opinions that I held of thee,

I credited thee with a soul of honour,

And should be loath to think I err'd therein :

Then, prythee, cease thy suit.—Thou seek'st my love,

And hast but barely 'scaped the plain reverse,

My scorn : thus in a heart that's wisely ruled,

Affection should be cured.

  *Esm.*      It lies too deep :

Contempt may cure a surface-shown desire,

But true love is enthroned beyond reproof.

  *Eth.* Thou feelest it, indeed.   Now, would my heart

Spoke not within me such a hopeless no !

Take comfort : fairer women are than I,

Milder in speech, and far more beautiful ;

And, from the ruins of thy present love,

Shall rise another of more auspices.

*Esm.* Oh, couldst thou know the inly fire of love,

How modestly it creeps into the heart,

And there, by secret, mute, and happy feeding,

Continually doth augment itself

Till reason have no pow'r to quench the flame,

Nay, rather joins her precious influence!

Alas! how wilt thou comfort my sick soul,

That dieth for thy love, thy love denied?

E'en as the leech, who with all drugs of earth

Encounters poison, save the antidote.

Grant me thy love, if thou wilt comfort me,

Which is more sweet and sov'reign to my soul,

Than cool redemption to a parchèd tongue.

*Eth.* I counsel thee, go from us for a season:

Time be thy nurse, whose light o'erpassing hand

Sows comfort and relief in ev'rything;

In darkness, day; sweet Summer's bounteous smile

Under the shaggy brow of Winter drear;

And, with the music of her rolling years,

Lulls sorrow into dim forgetfulness.

*Esm.* If ever Time shall darken o'er this flame,

Which memory shall feed till my death's hour;

If e'er mine eye let slip a wanton look,

Or my heart sigh for other earthly thing,

Say, I ne'er lov'd thee : hold me for a jest,

A reed, a weathercock, and no true man.

*Eth.* Though modesty should blush to see me so

Outstep a maiden's limit, still will I

Essay once more to be thy counsellor.

Waste not thy youth upon an idle chase ;

Quench not thy valour in the depths of love :

The boundless ocean hath more ports than one,

And he who from one haven is thrust back

To toss upon the weary boist'rous sea,

Doth wisely steer in search of peace elsewhere.

I counsel thee, go from us for a season :

Search out the world ; be look'd on ; air thy parts

Of honour in bright eyes and princely courts :

Ambition, be thy mark ; I say, press on ;

Set all thine heart thereto, and greatly win.

What, is't not more becoming to a man

To win bright glory from the gen'ral mouth,

Than to lie tangled in a lady's chain,

Pamp'ring his own despair ?    Go forth, I say :

Free    breath,    for    fainting    sorrow !    Soon    thou'lt
        find

This variously shifting scene of life

Blow up the spark in thy pale drooping soul,

And ope thine eyes on new affections.

 Tis true, alas ! thou art my father's staff,

His castle's rock, and, of his mut'nous men

Alone the forceful bond of unity,—

Still go, and Heav'n be with thee, as with us !

'Tis said, the harvest hath been plentiful

In the home-country, and the full-fed Danes

May haply give the world some breathing time :

There is no mention now of plunderers ;

Seize th' opportunity.

*Esm.*          I will not go.

Thou know'st, I cannot live apart from thee.

But see, the night hath fall'n, while we have talk'd ;

And through the thin rear of yon drifting clouds

The stars peep wickedly. Mischief's abroad

And couples with the wolf this fearful night.

How wild the wind amid the branches roars !

A storm frowns o'er the forest. Thunder ! Hark !

    *Enter* HOSKOLD *and another ; the latter seizes*

        ETHELBURGA.

*Eth.* What men are these ? Help me ; help,

      Esmund, help !

         *Enter* EDWIN *and Men.*

*Edw.* Am I too late ? Fellow, release that lady :

What, wilt thou fight ? Thy blood be on thyself.

             [EDW. *fights the man, who falls.*

*Hos.* Fly, quick.            [*To* ESMUND.

*Esm.*         Hast thou betray'd me ?

*Hos.*                                        No, by Heav'n!

*Esm.* I have a troop observing by the wood :

Let's steal away, and bring them to the rescue.

                              [Esm. *and* Hos. *steal away.*

*Edw.* Secure that man, and bring him to our

quarters.

Go, some of you, pursue the guilty squire :

My anger shall be hot, if he escape.      [*Exeunt Men.*

Now sweet thoughts to my heart, sweet utterance

Flow musically from my skilless tongue,

To cheer this pretty trembler : here she stands,

Her sweet pale face betwixt two lilies buried.

O God ! she needs must be most beautiful,

For beauty, like a daughter of the skies,

Ere she be seen, doth make her presence felt,

In trem'lous music o'er the spirit's chords.

Alas, would she but look upon me once !—

O heav'nly spirit of perfection,

Art thou descended upon earth ?   Bright soul !—

For grosser thing, I deem, thou canst not be,—

That art more beautiful than a saint's thought,

So holy, pure, and unexampled fair !

Oh, droop thy face no longer to the ground,

Lest the fond earth that roots the summer flow'r

Mistake thee for the pride of all her wreath,

And so embrace thee as her fairest child ;

But lift thine eyes, and sun those cheeks of snow,

Thou image of pale Dian, white with fear

And paler than the stilly midnight wave

Whereon the moonbeam trembles.   Does she hear me ?—

Rash man, I am her terror !   See, she lifts

Her eyes, and, meeting mine, droops them, as swift

As two faint stars that twinkle through the dark

And instantly retrieve themselves in night.

Sweet lady, let me do thee reverence.

*Eth.* I'm in thy pow'r : I fear, thou'rt mocking me.
I pray thee, do not kill me.

*Edw.*                    No, good sooth.

*Eth.* For there are those will pay thee hand-
somely.

*Edw.* All worldly riches being summ'd in thee

Must beggar all thy kin.  O lady, lady,

Since I have wrought some service for thy sake,

So let mine eyes some satisfaction take.

Wilt thou not look upon me once again ?

*Eth.* Was't thou came to my rescue ?

*Edw.*                                    Ay, sweet maid,

From rude enforcement of unholy men.

*Eth.* I thought thou wert a robber.

*Edw.*                               In mine eyes

Are two fond thieves that would thine image steal,

To be the goddess of an empty shrine :

My heart hath long been desolate for thee.

*Eth.* I do not think I fear thee very much :

Methinks a robber should not look as thou :

Oh, if thy soul be of a piece with thee,

Stain not her beauty with a cruel deed :

Be gentle, for thy looks' sake.

*Edw.* By all the pow'rs that mortal faith o'ersee,

By thy dear self, which is the greater oath,—

*Eth.* What man was that,—O me!—what man
    was he,

Who shamed my waist with his embracing arm ?

Oh, he did fright me, like a basilisk :

I would, I might forget his dreadful looks.

    *Edw.* He shall not live to frighten thee again.

    *Eth.* Nay, harm him not, I charge, or mine's the
    pain.

But say, how cam'st thou hither, or what saint

Wafted thee from the farthest end of earth ?

    *Edw.* Heav'n, and pure breezes that eschew offence,

Did waft the plot into my timely ear ;

Forthwith I called my men, came quickly hither,

And thus thy rescue was accomplishèd.

    *Eth.* I thank thee from my heart.    Teach me thy
    name,

That in my pray'rs I may remember it.

    *Edw.* Recall me by what name thou lovest best.

    *Eth.* Thine own were very well, if I knew that.

    *Edw.* Sweet, I am nameless, till thou christen me :

That name I bore, my heart hath put away

With an eternal, deeply-sworn divorce ;

For, I remember (oh, that this should be !)

That name was with thy race at enmity.

   *Eth.* I'd rather that thou wert a robber now ;

Be one, that I may buy thy heart of thee,

With all the wealth I have.

   *Edw.*                Give me thy glove ;

I'll wear it in my helm ; and he, who wins it,

Shall wear my poor life too.

<br>

            *Enter* THEODORE.

   *The.* My lord, a troop comes riding like the wind,

Bristling with spears and shining o'er with steel :

In the firm front the crafty squire doth ride,

Beside himself with rage ; his frown of thunder

Makes answer to the lightnings of his sword,

With which he cuts the air.

   *Edw.*           Lady, dear lady,

Time has run out for love's sweet circumstance,

So, to the centre of 't: I love thee!   Dost thou hear?

And wilt thou understand me what I mean,

When I do simply tell thee that I love thee?

And wilt thou in thine heart think o'er my love?

And wilt thou put an ocean in that word,

Of oaths and vows, and think I pour'd it forth?   .

 *Eth*. I fear thy love's too sudden: for they say,

That true love grows not in a single day.

 *Edw*. I would there were an oath of that fine pow'r,

As would enforce belief by hearing it.

Might I but stay, I have such reasons—oh!

Such wealth of terms to gild my love withal,

Thou shouldst perceive it, like the sun in Heav'n:

But now 'twere death.   Hark! they are calling thee.

 *Esm*. My lady!      [*Within*.

 *Edw*. Though I'm alone, I'll not relinquish thee

To that base man.

 *Eric*.    Ho! Lady Ethelburga! [*Within*.

 *Eth*. 'Tis Eric's voice: my father's henchman calls.

 *Eric*. My lady!      [*Within*.

*Edw.*          Sweet, farewell ; and think on me :

I will contrive some means to see thee soon ;

Oh, speedily I will.

*Eth.*          Farewell.                    *Going.*

*Edw.*               Farewell.

*Eth.* My soul returns, and wings me back to

      thee,                              *Returning.*

To say,—oh, yet I should not,—youth, though I

Know not thy name, my heart knows that I love thee :

Thou lov'st me too, thou say'st, and I believe thee,

Because to doubt, were pain.    Well, well ; thou dost :

Truth's in thine eye, and shall dispense with oaths.

*Edw.* Yet let me register my true love's vow

Upon this tablet of fair ivory,

Which, if I forfeit, may I ne'er know bliss ;

And thus I seal my soul's oath with a kiss.

*Esm.* My lady !                         [*Within.*

*Eth.*          They're at hand.    No more, no

      more.                               [*Exit.*

*Edw.* It is my soul, that leaves me thus alone,

4

Then farewell, life ; end with my date of joy.

As one who, from a sweet and happy dream,

Far straying in some lonely ocean-isle,

Wakes suddenly to find his ship a speck

Fading far off at sea, and wrings his hands,

The while with careless, quick, distracted feet,

He treads the desert, sad, sea-beaten shore,

E'en so am I : now, solitude, I know thee,

Even to suffocation : I could weep.

 *The.* For sorrow ?

 *Edw.*    No, for joy : and yet not that ;

My joy 's away.   O Time, thou heart of ice !

Thou cruel, mute, slow, pleasure-quenching fiend,

Couldst thou not kill me in the interval

That thou hast interposed 'twixt life and life ?

But let me cast about to find some means

To gaze once more upon this paragon.

Be fav'rable, thou supreme God of hearts !

Thou babe of inspiration, shine in me

With all thy subtle, wise, discerning fire ;

Make me an angel of intelligence,

To plot the sweet encounter of my love.

Hist, Theodore!

 *The.*   What is it, my good lord?

 *Edw.* Bring me the clothes of that hoar-headed Dane

Who died awhile since in our company.

Dost recollect him, boy? He was a man

All white with age, and silver-bleach'd by Time.

His beard flow'd to his waist; beyond his feet

Jutted his wrinkled face, so crook'd he was:

With staff in 's palsy-shaken hands, he limp'd

Thus,—seest thou, boy?—with such a crumbling step.

His looks would thrill all men with ghostly awe:

I've seen young warriors bow their steel-clad strength,

And give themselves to God, chanced they to light

Upon the creeping presence of that man.

Young Cupid shrive me for the sin, if I,

Who am a soldier listed in Love's wars,

Abuse my youth, to shut my warm blood up

In such an impotent receptacle.

There's more protection in a few gray hairs

Than in the steel proof of a coat of mail.

Thus mask'd, I'll enter in Lord Osric's castle,

And feast my soul upon this breathing pearl

That hangs in Danger's check.

    *The.*                         Oh, dear my lord,

Be not too rash.

    *Edw.*          Comfort, sweet Theodore!

For, pretty boy, when I have won my love,

I will prefer thee to become her page;

That, in the sunshine of her glorious eye,

Thou may'st for ever bask.   But truce to words!

For the swift hours are but shod with lead,

Until my feet are wing'd towards my love.

# ACT II.

## SCENE I.

### A CHAMBER IN LORD OSRIC'S CASTLE.

*Enter* Esmund.

*Esm.*  Crosses that put some weaker from their
    ends,

Breed but new fires in me.   Still to pursue,

As mortals may, is to o'ercome; so then

Fly on, ye swift desires; on, burning thoughts!

As falcons, to o'ertake your beauteous prey:

My soul no longer shall restrain your flight.

Let me consider then.   That stranger, sure,

Whom some mischance thrust in 'twixt me and

    bliss,

Should be the wide-reputed Saxon chief

Of whose arrival in these woods I hear,

And rumour doth report he claims this castle.

'Tis well, 'tis happy, 'tis most fortunate ;

For my Lord Osric, being old and weak

And shatter'd with severe infirmities,

Hath for these many years devolved on me

All warlike matters.   Of his former troop

Few live that now remember him ; while I,

From time to time, have fill'd the gaps with men

Devoted all to me.   Then here's my plan :

First, will I break upon Lord Osric's sleep,

And rouse his numb age with the fearful sight

Of this same threat'ning Saxon ; on which vantage,

I will entreat him strongly for his daughter,

Who haply then may more submissive prove,

Out of pure pity for her helpless sire.

If not,—farewell to conscience !   I'll seek out

The Saxon, and propose my love shall be

The costly purchase of my treachery.                    [*Exit.*

## SCENE II.

### ANOTHER CHAMBER IN THE CASTLE.

*Enter* Osric *and* Eric.

*Eric.* How fares my lord, to-day ?

*Osr.*                              Why, Eric, well ;

Better than old men use : thou know'st, my youth

Was not bestow'd on pleasure, therefore I

Do reap the fruits of honour in mine age.

*Eric.* And carry out the harvest bravely too :

Why, you should not be far off seventy ?

*Osr.* But seventy ?   Why, I remember me,

So many years back, for a boy of ten.

I'm eighty, Eric, though thou'lt not believe me.

*Eric.* No, no.

*Osr.*              'Tis true, howe'er thou think it strange :

Go, ask my liegemen, if thou doubt my lips,

Who have fought with me, and confess'd me lord,

Since first young Osric slipp'd his leading-strings.

But see, the sun hath seized on yonder wall ;

Support me to the window : 'tis most sweet

To look on nature at this budding time.

Sweet breath of spring, how thou renewest me !

    *Eric.* Here you may have a fair and distant view.

    *Osr.* The rosy morn, upon the hills uprous'd,

Brushes the dewy lawn with flying feet,

Descending to the plain : the dappled clouds

Course o'er the flow'ry fields ; the light bee hums

In the shy bosom of the blushing rose.

Hark, Eric, how the lark his matin sings,

Far risen in you deep blue crystalline ;

His chorus, all creation, full and strong.

The hounds are forth upon the distant hills,

With eager bay rousing the noble chase ;

The horn winds through the dell ; the forest glades

Ring gaily with the whistling woodman's stroke ;

The ploughman's smack is heard, and hearty voice,

Urging his oxen through the cloddy fields ;

And see, reflected in the sleeping lake,

The snowy breast of you proud-sailing cloud,

That o'er its mirror stoops, and hovers there,

To gaze on its own virgin majesty.

Sweet scene of beauty !   O perfection sole !

O bright reflection of celestial things !

How calm and gracious is thine influence,

How deep, and beyond utterance, thy pow'r !

Methinks, my veins swell with the tide of youth,

And that I am no more a weak old man,

The while I gaze on beauty.   Oh, she hath

A sov'reign spell to lift the weary soul

From this dark maze, wherein we, lost, do pine,

To happy mansions of immortal bliss,

Where only freedom dwells and true content.

Let him be envied of all grosser men,

Whose heart, not hooded o'er by worldliness,

Can truly feel this precious influence,

For he alone can know felicity.

'Tis an elixir of perpetual youth,

That, e'en beneath gray hairs, can save for us

The happy thrill of childhood, and beguile,

By repetition of familiar sights,

Our souls to the glad times when we were young.

Dost know, my Eric, I sometimes inquire,

Within myself, when on these scenes I gaze,

If all my middle life were not a dream.

I have breathed peace so long, that warlike thoughts

Seem but the memory of another world,

And marvel how this wither'd arm I lift,

Once grasped Lord Osric's sword, the fiery Dane,

Who tore this castle from its Saxon lord.

I am transported to my youth again,

By gazing on these old familiar sights,

By giving ear to these remembered sounds :

Thus sang the merry lark when I was young,

Thus joyfully would bark the nimble hounds ;

The breeze thus whisper'd, mid the summer leaves,

His amorous-complaining melody ;

And thus in youth the brook flow'd silverly.

    *Eric.* What, is Lord Osric old ?   Not so ; old age

We measure not by counting of our years,

Nor by the snows bedrizzled on our heads,

But by the infirm soul.   Could you but hear

The trump of war!   Ah! there's Lord Osric's vein.

   *Osr.* Eric, thou'rt old to be a flatterer.

   *Eric.* 'Tis but your modesty that calls me so,

For uttering an universal truth.

   *Osr.* There was a thing that troubled me last night;

'T has slipp'd my memory.

   *Eric.*               Why, this it was:

My lady Ethelburga stay'd from home;

'Twas nightfall, and a storm raged o'er the wood,

Was terrible to see.

   *Osr.*          When came she back?

   *Eric.* Ere midnight, safe.   To tell a foolish tale,

That should be chidden on an old man's tongue;—

The storm, for shame to have so rudely beat

Upon so fair a creature in his wrath,

To show his dumb contrition to the maid,

On either cheek had hung a wat'ry pearl,

As speaking-precious as an angel's tear.

*Osr.* What escort had she with her?   Didst thou see?

*Eric.* An armèd company : 'twas so, in truth.

*Osr.* Why so?

*Eric.*          In happy time here comes your squire :
Sir Esmund will inform you of those things.


*Enter* ESMUND, *in haste.*


*Esm.* Good morrow to your lordship.   Here's a morn
To bring fresh roses into wither'd cheeks :
By Heav'n ! it fills my soul with luxury :
As balmy, thrilling, and restorative,
To those who feel their current on the ebb,
As that fair Shunnamite, whose sweet young breath
Fann'd David's cheek, as on his breast she lay.
You've risen early.

*Osr.*          Esmund, what's thy news ?
Not peaceful, for I see thine armour's on :
And such a forc'd smile plays upon thy brow,
As when the sun strikes through embattled clouds.
Smile all, or be all frowns ; be peace or war.

And why dost thou approach so hastily?

I am no soldier, if some mischief lurks not

Under so hot a tread.

 *Esm.*    Regard it not,

My lord.—This message, Eric, to the men.—

         [*Exit* ERIC.

And yet in truth I could have wish'd I had

A tale more fit for venerable ears.

 *Osr.* Away, this shy beginning of rough things!

This soft and maidenlike exordium,

That ushers in the flaming majesty

Of glorious war!  Forgett'st thou who I am?

Osric, am I, a soldier, and a Dane.

How dar'st thou preface to me I am old,

When thy next word's of war?  I know it, I.

What! think'st thou I've no strength?—Within there,

 Eric!

Bring me my weapon from the armoury.—

I'll show thee in a trice, what I can do.

 *Esm.* Oh, sir, content you for a little space.

*Osr.* I've slept too long of late ; I own 't, with shame :

In peace, a soldier grows luxurious :

But 'twas occasion for mine arms that slept,

And not my need, that wink'd on exigence.

Peruse my person o'er : are these the limbs,

That usually accompany old age ?

'Tis luxury that drains the strength of man,

And rots him ere the timely stroke of death.

In the first fire of impetuous youth,

And when my weightier arm proclaim'd me man,

'Twas still my glory to be first afield :

With all my soul I did attend upon

The shrill-sped summons of ennobling war ;

Yea, my heart hung upon it, as its food :

And now I'm old, shall I forget myself ?

Then Osric were not Osric, but his tomb,

And lives to chronicle a man that's dead.

I tell thee, Esmund, when I hear that note,

By day, or stretch'd upon my bed at night,

If but one limb can to the other move,

Or stand at all, old Osric shalt thou see
Helm his gray hairs to do a martial deed,
Arm his scarr'd breast, and to the battle ride,
Through banded shields to pierce to his brave sire,
Who from the blessed halls of Odin show'rs
Sweet looks upon brave deeds.

*Esm.*                              Had I been told,
Or had I dream'd there lay so fresh a soul
Under that white and wrinkled bark of life,
I still had doubted it.   Oh, I want words
To meet this marvel!   To the saints be praise,
That have prolong'd your vigour with your days.
Your valour shall have speedy breath, my lord.
I hope, I've not offended.

*Osr.*                    Oh, no, no!
Esmund, I love thee well ; I know thee for
An honest and a right brave gentleman.
But, prythee, keep me in suspense no more.

*Esm.* Thus rumour doth report : a Saxon lord
Hath lately with a troop possessed the forest ;

'Tis said, moreover, that he claims your castle.

This hearing, I (oh, pardon it) concealed ;

Partly, for rumour is a liar approved,

But chiefly, that I fear'd t' imperil you,

Being old, with such fierce news ; though I was wrong
     there :

But truth spoke out last night ; for as my lady,

Guarded by me, pass'd homeward in the dusk,

Some men sprang from an ambush suddenly,

And seized your daughter.   On the instant, I

Drew, and defended her ; but being press'd

By many weapons, and my lady in act

To be borne off, and knowing that a troop

Was station'd near, I ran with all my strength,

And brought them in ; at whose approach, the men

Fled for their lives, and left your daughter harmless.

   *Osr.*  Now by my sword, if I have closed mine
     eyes

That robbers may o'erleap the pales of law,

And ravish in the face of open day,—

What, 'neath the very frown of this my castle !—

I am unworthy to have lived so long.

*Esm.* My reputation to a jester's bell,

If these were robbers !   O my lord, not so :

I know what kind of creature is a thief ;

Pale, stealthy, timorous, brave but by night,

Slinking, like ghosts, from day : but these were men,

Whose faces were as open title-deeds

Writ to all present and to future times,

By nature's hand sealed with her ruddiest blood

Unto possession of this fair round earth,

And for a name, term'd Saxons.   See, my lord ;

Here comes one to confirm me.


*Enter* OSWITH.

*Osw.*                    To Lord Osric,

Mine embassy.

*Osr.*        Lord Osric hears you, herald.

Say first, who sent you.

*Osw.*              From Lord Edwin, I

5

Bear this demand ; either restore this castle,

Now my Lord Edwin's, by inheritance

From his deceased sire, Lord Ethelwulf :

And whereof he, the said Lord Ethelwulf,

Was formerly disseized by violence ;

Or, failing this condition, name a day

Whereon, supported by what pow'r you have,

You may oppose Lord Edwin in the field,

And, to award of the just God of battles,

Submit your title ; which to be conceived

In the set teeth of justice, law and honour,

My master now avers, and, trusting to

That high imperial Pow'r who ever arms

Right with His majesty, sends you, by me,

Defiance, with this glove.

  *Osr.*       A moment, stay.

I ask thee, herald, is thy lord a knight ?

  *Osw.* By the hand of Richard, Duke of Normandy.

  *Osr.* Why then, Sir Esmund, take the challenge up ;

And, gentle herald, bear this answer back :

Since, without God inspire, our actions all

Are weak and nerveless as an infant's arm,

Nay, wither'd ere conceived in our will's womb,

So by His aid did I obtain this castle,

And so by His continuing grace will I

Retain 't ; so let thy lord consider well

How he array himself against a man

So prosperous and well with God as me.

But if thy master, in contempt of life,

Would spit himself into the jaws of death,

And drag his comrades after (whose sad state

Moves me to tears), Lord Osric's wont is not

To baulk a foe in the pursuit of glory.

When honour calls him, and his fame's at stake,

A man must loose the bonds of charity,

And from his bosom thrust each kindly thought

To wither in the fiery sun of war ;

Till, in the eve of the contention's heat,

His foe upon the green cool turf doth lie,

And to compassion of a brave man fall'n,

Unseals the parch'd fount of the victor's tears.

Tell him, in fine,

Lord Osric, on the seventh day, will dare

His utmost valour upon Brackley moor.

 *Osw.* Nobly deliver'd ! As the bird of Jove

Gives warning of a king, so flying Fame,

That through all Christian countries spoke of you,

Advised us of a brave and courteous knight.

Accept my thanks, and with th' assurance you

Find in your breast, credit Lord Edwin too.

 *Osr.* This chain of gold was once a Swedish knight's,

Whom on the plains of Germany I slew.

Ah, rest his soul ! he was a gallant man ;

His fellow lives not now. Wear't for me, sir.

 *Osw.* I thank your lordship, and so take my leave.

 *Osr.* Farewell, sir, and commend me to your lord.

[Exit OSWITH.

I never heard a man more dignify

Himself in speech. If but the oracle

Shame not his mouthpiece, this young Saxon lord

Were worthier to live Lord Osric's friend

Than perish by his sword.   Spirit of battles,

Thou true Promethean spark, how thou rekindlest

Cold nature in my limbs !   But now, I was

As one benumbed with winter, reft of soul,

Heavy and sapless as a fallen tree ;

Now my blood dances like a spring-touch'd brook.

I think, life hath her seasons circling round,

And youth comes in upon the rear of age.—

O God ! I thank thee, that Thou hast vouchsafed

Some glory still to my far-travell'd sun,

Ere it decline to its dark western tomb.—

What ! rouse thee, Esmund : is thy joy so mute ?

Oh, then, thou'lt weep upon thy wedding day.

Why hang'st thou thy sad head so leadenly ?

And bit'st thy lip ?   Man of my heart, what ails

   thee ?

Art thou translated into Osric's body ?

Thou hast a look of age.

  *Esm.*     And reason for it :

When Wisdom is by old men thrust away,

Fain must she dwell with youths.

   *Osr.*                        I see, thine eye

Labours with meaning.   O' my faith, I'll 'scape thee :

I'll not be midwife to so wise a babe.

Thou art too prudent to be merry, sir,

When merriment's becoming.   I'll at once

Go forth, and marshal all my warriors.—

Nay, speak, man, if thou wilt ; discharge that look.

   *Esm.* My lord, my lord, could words to weapons turn,

Or valour in one breast rout a whole army,

Against all men, yours were the victory.

But oh, bethink you of your humble means

To follow these proud thoughts.   Alas ! how slowly

Performance limps after our wingèd wills.

Your men are few in number, lazy, proud,

Gross-bodied, feeble, mut'nous to the core,

And from the bloody clasp of war long free,

Are fall'n asunder through lax discipline.

Horses, and arms, and warlike furniture

Are more defective than you can suppose.

Ah, my dear master, that I should say this!

But when your heart finds this brave utterance,

Mine own refuses to respond Amen.

    *Osr.* Now, for mine honour's sake, I must reprove thee.

Had I not proved thee by experience

To be beyond suspicion a brave man,

I'd tell thee to thy face, " There spoke a coward."

What man who lives, or from his grave can boast

That e'er he took Lord Osric at surprise?

Hast thou not heard me tell of the Lord Stein?

    *Esm.* Alas! my lord.

    *Osr.*               I think thou dost forget.

In Denmark, on a time, my castle stood

Perch'd on the swart brow of a pine-clad rock;

And the Redhand (for so they call'd Lord Stein)

In the still hours came suddenly upon me.

Jesu! was war within the skies that night:

The wind did battle with the chimney-stalks,

Hurling them from the roof; the gaunt trees roar'd,

And toss'd their mighty branches to and fro,

Contending in their strength ; near and more near

The iron step of Thor roll'd o'er the hills,

Shaking the vault of heav'n ; and, in the midst,

Fearfully quench'd, the lamp of night went out,

And darkness swallow'd up both earth and sky.

But from the casement of my castle-keep

As through the gloom I gazed, a single flash

Tore the obscurity ; was something moved,

And glitter'd in the light ; I knew 'twas arms :

I rous'd my men ; in silence deep we arm'd,

And secret watch'd behind the close-barr'd gates.

Softly our foes came climbing up the steep,

From crag to crag ; full eighty men in steel :

But when now half was gather'd at the edge,

We drew the bolt, and with a cry rush'd forth.

Then o'er the thunder rose the din of war ;

Shout answer'd shout, and arms rang horribly :

The screams of falling men appall'd the night,

Remorselessly hurl'd o'er the steep incline.

Flamed o'er with a pine-torch, the Redhand stood ;

He raised his battle-axe, and rush'd at me :

Sweyn took the blow upon his lifted targe,

And, flashing round, my great two-handed sword

Descended on his shoulder ; low he fell :

Then turn'd his men, and, leaping down the rock,

Fled cow'ring o'er the plain, their recreant backs

Turn'd to the pale eye of the tim'rous moon.—

We bore him swiftly through the castle gates,

Unarm'd him tenderly, and laid him down

On mine own couch.  Alas ! thrice gallant foe,

Wast then, alas ! wast then a dying man,

Though all the glories of Walhalla shone

In thy bright hero's eyes.  Softly my hand

Thou took'st in thine, and with a sigh that bore

Thy spirit on its wings, thus murmur'd forth :

" Thy castle, my Lord Osric,

" Is like a thunder-cloud, wherein Jove sits,

" That, being but reach'd at by ambitious hand,

" Doth shoot forth instant death."  His eyes grew dim,

And his brave spirit was in happiness.—

O Esmund, in those days were men indeed!

But for these shallow youths of Saxony,—

The very spawn of these degen'rate times,—

'Tis but to don our steel-coats and ride forth,

Or, like the famous Greek, great Peleus' son,

Peep o'er the battlements and shout at them,

And further they'll not stay.

    *Esm.*               Oh, that a man

By too much courage should undo himself,

And by assurance arm his enemy!

Oh, rouse thee, gallant lord; shake off this dream:

Time runneth on the while your thoughts sleep fast.

Prosperity is in the hand of Heav'n,

And earthly fortunes are as shifting sand.

    *Osr.* Hath anything befallen to my men?

Why, think; 'twas but the other day I storm'd

This castle with a regiment of fire.

    *Esm.* Pardon, my lord; 'twas twenty years now since;

And of your men most part are in their graves:

Some few still linger in the eye of Death,

Who, like a gaoler, in their footsteps walks,

Stealing his shadow o'er them ere himself:

Pale, feeble, toothless, sunken in their cheeks,

Some blind, some deaf, some wanting of a limb,

And scarce a soul but drivels in his talk :

E'en as the last few wither'd leaves of Autumn,

Left to bewail their too long living hap,

While Winter, stern and pale, comes frowning in ;

Grey ghosts of strength, mere memories of men,

Stray gleanings from the busy hand of Fate.

   *Osr.* Was it so long ?    Oh, let me pause awhile.

But wilt thou tell me it was twenty years ?

Yet let me think :—Oh, yes, oh, yes ! it was :

O memory ! O Osric ! fallen ! fallen !

Vain-glorious man, what dost thou meditate ?

Thou quenchèd light, wilt thou be flaming still,

And glitter in the front of warriors ?

Osric, thou hast grown old : thine hairs are grey ;

Thy brain hath turn'd to folly.

*Esm.*                    Give me leave——

*Osr.* Nay, Esmund, I have done with flattery.

Whom sorrow teaches, learns his lesson well.

Those sweet delusions of old age have fled,

And cleared mine eyes, that now I see these limbs

Are wither'd, halt, and feeble.

*Esm.*                    I but thought

To check you flying madly, not to bring

That lofty and thrice noble spirit to earth,

Pierc'd with so sharp a pang.   Do I not love you ?

*Osr.* I know thou dost, my Esmund, and I turn

To thee more confidently in that thought.

Listen : my life hath met with some applause ;

I have reaped glory with a sweating brow,

And fame so earned is sweet, sweeter than life.

Should this young Saxon come upon me now,

When I am feeble and enthrall'd by age,

Fast bound in sickness and infirmities,

And, pilf'ring from me mine illustrious name,

Leave me defenceless to the cruel tongue

That stings misfortune to the quick !   O Esmund,

In one disgrace, ingloriously slain,

Should Osric and his honour lie entombed.

*Esm.* Far, far, my noble master, be such end

To such a life.

*Osr.*          Look, Esmund, on thy youth

I lean the burden of my fourscore years :

Staff up mine ancient honour, lest it fall,

And bear me to my grave.

*Esm.*              And so I will ;

And, with His aid, who fights for a just cause,

Will bring you honourably through this strife.

Yet longs my heart to utter a request.

*Osr.* What Osric and his honour can accord,

Be sure is thine.

*Esm.*          Oh, let me be forgiv'n,

If in this hour I shall presume too far

Upon my vantage.   You, my lord, have oft,

When I improved your men in martial arts,

Both praised my skill and heaped me up with thanks

For its unbought bestowal.  Many years

Have I served you with many services,

Nor asked reward.  When danger threaten'd you,

Mine eyes have wearied out the starry night,

To watch the coming of your enemies ;

And oft (for now I dare confess so much)

That your grey head might know tranquillity,

And nightly on a quiet pillow lie,

Have I, unknown, join'd battle with your foes,

Fought secretly, and without glory conquer'd.

  *Osr.*  For which I could desire myself more rich

Of recompence.

  *Esm.*   And I myself more rich

A thousand thousand times in services

To merit that I ask ; which, if you grant,

Both beggars me of claim and runs before

To make my future bankrupt.  Ah, my lord !

Seeing that all men serve for recompence,

And without motive, none, for what serve I ?

What object have I set before mine eyes,

Whose wished consummation nerves my limbs

To labour in the painful race of life ?

Thyself dost know (who trulier than thou ?)

What witchery beams from the eye of Fame,

Who, in the vision of all noble spirits,

Stands vested in a thousand heav'nly hues.

Some desire knowledge ; 'tis a godlike thirst ;

And earthlier spirits burrow still for gold.

But me, thou seest, by nor fame nor wealth

Enthrall'd, nor the request of learning sweet :

The prize is still to find, that lures me on.

What fancy sprung of earth or air seek I ?

Oh, scorn me not, because I answer, love ;

Ah ! fame and wealth are shadows to pursue ;

For who can clasp them to his beating heart,

And rest content ?   But 'tis not so with love ;

That hath a form and beauty palpable,

To gaze upon, touch, circle, and enjoy,

Till drowned bliss wake in Elysium,

And turn to his celestial food again.

Who seeketh fame, must walk companionless ;

But sweet society attends on love.

Wisdom still treads upon a precipice,

And oft with thought grown giddy and brainsick,

Down topples into moody discontent :

But he who loves, and is in turn beloved,

Lock'd up and bosom'd in his own content,

Looks from the shelter of a happy heart,

And with unenvious eye sees Folly throned,

And robed in honours proudly bear herself ;

In sweet and inward contemplation wrapt

Above the thoughts of sad mortality.

Ah me ! what gold, digg'd from the depths of hell,

Shall be compared with Love's golden locks ?

What glory, harp'd upon strange lips, outweigh

The sweet report writ in Love's beaming eye ?

In presence of the king, what fool were he

Should court the lent light of the minister !

E'en so the man, who woos Philosophy,

Nor first does homage at the shrine of Love,

Who oft the risen soul hurls from his seat,

And bends his proud neck to entreat a child.

But when adorèd Love dwells in a man,

And sways the fury of his warring thoughts,

Oh, then, his fancy, from brute sense refined,

On viewless wings cleaving the liquid sky,

Can soar beyond the eagle in her flight,

And pass the swallow that wings o'er the sea.

Yea, oft such vigour is in mortal man,

When through his chaste eye Love on beauty looks,

From thought to thought, from bliss to bliss led on

Through a succession of bright images,

Into the imperishable sea he breaks,

To visions in immortal glory bathed,

Where Justice, Temperance, and Virtue dwell,

Hymning sweet music to the ear of Heav'n:

So spake the holiest man of ancient Greece,

Wise Socrates, upon whose shoulder sate

Apollo, in the likeness of a dove,

And whisper'd oracles into his ear.

Ah me! to laud so sweet a sovereign

I have a mint of phrases in my brain;

But the swift feet of all-too-nimble Time

Fast follow on my breathless fluency

And bid me thus to sum mine argument,—

That he who wealth desires or earthly fame,

Seeks but a shadow, a mere gilded name;

But he who after Love his footsteps bends,

He travels on the road in bliss that ends.

*Osr.* Assuredly some god possesses thee;

'Tis not thyself who speaks, but he through thee.

But name to me the lady of thy heart.

*Esm.* My lord, she is your daughter, Ethelburga.

*Osr.* Ha! this proves me more blind than I am halt,

Else surely had mine eyes discern'd so far.

Alas! I fear thy suit's impossible.

Why, man, she is a marriage for a king:

I have had offers—Oh, she is the star,

The polar star, of gazing noblemen,

By whom his heart's affections each doth steer.

Full many an honour'd knight—ay, that he has—

Hath sought her hand, and for her favour swore

To rid the world of Turks, yea, to perplex

Hell with slain heretics ; but, being old,

I could not bring myself to part from her,

That she should vanish from me utterly.

    *Esm.* Heav'n knows, as I would have you think, my

        lord,

I never thought to prosper in this suit.

Fortune hath not so smiled upon my life,

That my heart's hopes are swell'd with insolence ;

But as a sick man tells to all the world

The tedious story of his sufferings,

Without respect of who can cure his pain,

E'en so my sorrows did out-talk my hopes,

That, heavy with despair, still droop'd behind.

And yet I would those words were still to say,

Which have put separation 'twixt us two.

Now forth I go, to wander through the world,

And seek for comfort where no comfort is.

Farewell, my lord ; henceforth account me dead ;

For so I am, my light of life being fled.

   *Osr.* Why, look, I did not bid thee to despair :

Jesu ! how swift of thought these lovers are !

Esmund, were I to grant thy wishes now,

When I am old and hardly borne upon,

Some men might say I chose my interest

Rather than Esmund for my son-in-law :

And yet I swear to thee it is not so.

Though many men my daughter have desired,

Of all her suitors I esteem thee most,

And willingly would make her o'er to thee.

    *Esm.* My gracious lord ! what thanks have I for

      this ?

    *Osr.* But stay, first must I question her desires ;

For I so nicely weigh her happiness,

That if she but thy little finger hate,

Or take exception to a hair of thee,

No further mention must be of this match.

I will go presently, and talk with her.        [*Exit.*

*Esm.* Ay, go to her, and my soul go with thee,

To teach persuasion to thine aged lips.

The sire look from thine eyes, speak in thy tones,

And touch her bosom with authority!

Oh, may thy silver hairs and cruel needs

Move her to pity!   There are some would say

" 'Twere satisfaction small to lover's fire

To wed a wife that she might love her sire;"

But such ne'er loved; for who that does can look

Beyond possession of the thing he loves?

There thought, being quench'd in its own too much

      bliss,

Travels no further in futurity.

But if this hazard prove unlucky too,

Then to Lord Edwin I myself will hire,

And, with my soul, purchase my soul's desire.   [*Exit.*

## SCENE III.—BEFORE THE CASTLE GATES.

*Enter* EDWIN, *disguised as an aged Dane.*

*Edw.* Ye stately tow'rs, ye proud-eyed battlements,

Under whose bending brows suspicion shrinks,

And wraps him closer in his counterfeit!

Oh, yet again, I greet ye : hold ye still

Young Edwin in remembrance ?   I am he,

Though sadder by some twenty years than when

Ye saw my childhood.   Ah, debauch'd of Fortune !

Time-serving traitors, flatt'rers, summer-friends !

And could ye from a stranger ward the winds,

While he who own'd ye, loved ye, to the storm

Gave his unshelter'd head ?

Yet soft ; my love doth sanctify your guilt :

Guilt ! 'tis mine own, for branding ye with it,

Being usurp'd so sweetly : lightlier fold

My lady in your kind embracing guard

Than the close portals of the willing rose

The soft intrusion of the pretty bee.

While Edwin toss'd upon the weary deep,

Here cradled was his love, that is his soul;

Then may 't be said, he never roved at all:

How love can varnish o'er a bitter thought!—

But time slips by the meditative man,

That should be seiz'd to purpose.    Here's the horn

That parleys with this castle : at this blast

Fly Fortune to my aid.                    [*Winds the horn.*

*Enter* HOSKOLD.

*Hos.*                    Old man, what want you,

That thus you boldly dare the echoes wake?

*Edw.* Rest, and a morsel, sir, for Jesus' sake.

Look, I am old, and I have travell'd far:

The palsy 's in my limbs; see, how they shake:

My spirit faints for lack of nourishment.

*Hos.* Beggar, away! and to a convent hie;

Here's no besotted den of monkery.

*Edw.* A surly soul behind so fair a face!

Sweet beauty sourly marr'd is man's disgrace :

If thou wilt nature's favours not supplant,

Look not so darkly on a suppliant.

I prythee, let me in.

    *Hos.*           Begone, thou cheat ;

The flatt'ring tongue proclaims its own deceit.

My fingers 'gin to twine about my staff :

The hound hath smelt thee out ; hark, how he growls.

    *Edw.* Thou wilt not let him tear me ?

    *Hos.*                Yes, I will.

    *Edw.* I will amaze thee with some wondrous arts,

Which from the cunning Saracen I learn'd.

Such virtue can I breathe into a sword,

It shall cut stone ; but mace, nor battle-axe,

Swift-flying arrow, nor steel-headed lance,

Shall aught avail against thy coat of mail,

When I have charm'd it.

    *Hos.*          Let me see thy hand.

Fellow, where didst thou get that jewell'd ring ?

Thief, thou hast stolen it : give it to me.

*Edw.* What, scoundrel, what! dar'st thou call me a
thief?
I'll break thy head, to mend thy manners, boor.

[*Strikes him.*

*Hos.* Help! murder! within there!


*Enter several Retainers.*

*1st Ret.*                              Has the knave fled,
Who made thee roar so lustily to us?

*Hos.* The ancient hypocrite has three men's strength.

*2nd Ret.* Let see, if he be man or miracle:—
Come, snow-bedeck'd volcano, to thy staff.—
This is the prettiest match that e'er I saw.
A ring! a ring! stand round.

*Hos.*                              Ye are all fools:
Ye know, I fear him not.

*2nd Ret.*                              The ancient man
Hath still a nose to smell a coward out,
For all his looks of Jove, and big round voice.
A ring! a ring! Th' old man shall have fair play.

*1st Ret.* Be silent: see, Lord Osric comes this
way.

*Enter* OSRIC.

*Osr.* Peace, hounds! Unruly curs, who gave ye
leave
To bark down order by my castle gates ?
Off, to your work! Begone, ye idle knaves.—

*[Exeunt Retainers.*

Old man, why com'st thou here, to stir up strife
Among my people ?

*Edw.*                     Hear me, my good lord.
I did but crave your servant for some food,
To be repaid with labour of these hands,
(For yet I am not altogether weak,)
And with the account of some amazing arts
Practised in foreign countries, wherein I
Boast skill ; when he, this late prostrated rascal,
Branded me thief, which so unfroze my age,
I was a youth again.

*Osr.* Inhospitable boor, out of my sight! [*To* HOSKOLD.

Shall my repute be dimm'd for such as thee?

God knows how long, but yet the day's to come,

When to the wretched Osric bars his doors.—

Go, get thee in, old man; supply thy wants. [*Walks aside.*

*Hos.* This be the plaister to my smarting skull!

[*Aside.*

That mine eyes flash'd not to a soul that's dull:

Me with a feather my least babe subdue

Till I cry quarter, if this be not true;

No old man knock'd me then. The sun hath shone

On many a disguise before this one.

I'll to Sir Esmund, ere it be too late,

And show him Saxon written on my pate. [*Exit.*

*Osr.* Aid me, ye heav'nly pow'rs! give me not o'er

[*Aside.*

To ruin in mine age: with sweat and blood

Mine honours were acquired; let not another

Reap the ripe harvest of my painful youth.

*Edw.* This ancient man should be mine enemy: [*Aside.*

I thought him not so old.   Time ne'er look'd on

A braver record : though his strength be fall'n,

The soul of dignity, o'erspreading him,

Makes ruin glorious.   How with manliness

Is sweetness intertwined !   In his eyes glows

The setting majesty of world-wide honour.

An angry cloud mars his serenity ;

Something has ruffled him.

  *Osr.*     She loves him not, [*Aside.*

Or so she hinted ; further I'd not press her,

Lest my necessities should woo her, not

Her inclinations.   God ! 'tis pitiful

That the estate and honours of a man,

The scant reward of toil and many wounds,

Should in his weak old age be reft from him

For a girl's whim.   My fate's at Esmund's call ;

If he desert me at this pinch, I fall.

Heav'n's will be done !   Old man, why stay'st thou here ?

          [*To* EDWIN.

Go, get thee in.   Ha ! tarry : didst thou not

E'en now, upon a sudden spur of ire,

Level that swaggerer ?

*Edw.*  He soiled mine honour :

Foul-spoken knave, vituperative cur !

I would his lesson were to teach again ;

Under your pardon always, good my lord.

*Osr.*  Thou'rt wither'd, lame, old, seeming impotent :

Where gott'st thou strength for the puissant deed ?

*Edw.*  In honesty, my lord, and th' unquench'd fire

Of soul, that tamely ne'er put up with wrong.

This, the reserve on which an old man draws,

In the decay of sinews and brute flesh.——

Have I your pardon for it ?

*Osr.*                    Oh ! fear not :

I thought not to reprove thee ; rather thou

Deserv'st esteem.—Oh ! I am moved by this ;

And it hath turn'd the tide of sorrow back,

Wherein my manhood lay a-perishing.

If slight occasion and a trifling cause

Can rouse such virtue in a beggar's limbs,

Heavy and stiff with age, whose soul, belike,

Ne'er knew the honourable exercise

Of one high thought by which t' inspire anew

The wither'd sepulchre of mortal strength—

Being fretted to the shadow of a shadow

By care and poverty, shall Osric whine,

When peril looks at him, because he's old ?

Crave aid because his hands are sinewless ?

And bend his proud knee to his own esquire,

For lack of other recompence ?   Oh, wake !

Awake, thou soul of Osric, and cast off

This chain of years, which doth environ thee.

Forget, ye limbs, that Time, the cormorant,

Hath prey'd upon your rounded manliness.

Ye fingers, ye must learn again to fight.

Brighten, ye aged eyes, with one last gleam,

And then be quench'd in honour.   Hark, old man ;

                                        [*To* EDWIN.

How say'st thou ; wilt thou stay and serve with me ?

   *Edw.* Full weary am I of my wandering :

My feet are sore with tracing countries far;

So is my heart most sad and desolate

With measuring the vast unbounded sea :

Here gladly would I rest my feeble age

From the long sorrows of my pilgrimage.

   *Osr.* Doubt not thy welcome.   For thy first employ,

Go, seek the knave on whom thy rousèd hand

Scored salutation, and require of him

Mine armour, which bring hither.   I am fixed

                              [*Exit* EDWIN.

Not to ask aid I cannot recompense :

The love I bear to my true-thoughted squire,

Makes me to wish my daughter had as much.

Alas ! what tongue, though the sweet Attic bee

Flew from his thymy bow'r in the blest shades,

Or though Apollo spake, or lofty Jove,

Might, to her plain advantage, urge a woman ?

Yet, when the wooing's maddest to be heard,

Though priest and parent hang upon her gown

With weight of all their reasonable saws,

Her heart is lighter to be borne away

Than vagrant straws upon a gusty day.

But Heav'n so framed them, doubtless, with advice.

To force them to discretion, 'gainst their bent,

As ruffian fathers do (whom God requite!),

Were as to build in sand, steer the wild wind,

Or on the ocean force stability.

God's blessing with her! she shall please herself.

Brave Esmund hath my pity : I must meet

His sickness with employment.   At the court

Of Norman Richard stands my cousin high,

Count Robert ; to his care I will commend him.

O holy Odin! can this be my armour ?

            [*Enter* EDWIN *with armour,*

Come, rusty mirror, let me look on thee ;

Show Osric his chang'd self.

   *Edw.*                     It has lain by

For years.

   *Osr.*    For full fifteen.   Come, lace my greaves :—

Nay, 'tis too tight ; ah ! tenderly, I pray.

Soh !  now  my  mail ;  give  't  to  me  in  my
  hand.

*Edw.* Let me support you, or you will not stand.

*Osr.* Is this the sword, O Osric, thou didst wield,

And like Jove's angel flash'd o'er Saxon hosts ?—

Support me to you seat ; I'll rest awhile.    [*To* EDWIN.

How happy wert thou in thy low estate,

Fellow, didst thou but know 't !   Within thy face

A lecture's writ, that makes the reader sad :

Alas ! how oft have I remark'd thine eye,

Wherein thy soul did manifestly sit,

Scan o'er these walls, ah ! feast upon the stones,

Till envy with a sigh raised from thy depths

Brimm'd o'er thy cheek in brine.   I marvel much

How such a sordid and earth-bound desire

Inhabits still so reverend a man.

Couldst thou experience the cares of wealth !

The painful bridling of licentious youth,

The ceaseless toil of still-pursuing manhood,

And then the terrors of infirm old age

To be despoiled in his feebleness
Of all the winnings of his lustier years ;
Then haply wouldst thou bless thy poverty
That sings in presence of the highway thief.—
My helm !   Pull 't off, pull 't off ; I cannot breathe.

*Edw.* Some water, within there ! my lord is faint.

*Enter* ETHELBURGA, *with retainers.*

*Eth.* O saints and angels, what a sight is this !
The water ! give 't to me.   Keep back ; ye press
Too close about your lord ; give him more air.—
Sweet life, lift from thy bosom thy dear head,
And ope thine eyes again.

*Osr.*                          Ah, Ethelburga !

*Eth.* What evil, subtle, and designing man
(My worst ill wishes tend upon him still !)
Possess'd thee to affront those limbs, which nought
But reverence should clothe and soft attire,
With such a martial dress ?

*Osr.*                          Nay, prithee, cease :

Child, art thou mocking me, that art thyself

Cause of this exhibition of my folly?

*Eth.* What now you mean, I know not.

*Osr.*                                     Ay, thou'rt kind;

So wilt be to thy life's end : when I drop

Into my grave, though thou hast help'd me there,

Thou'lt kindly cover me.    'Tis in the voice

And manner of some women, this deceit;

But hath no more of kindred with their grain

Than the rose colour on their cheeks.

*Eth.*                                     My father,

Tell me, in what have I offended you.

*Osr.* Nay, but in nought, my sweet and gentle girl;

Forgive me, for my wits are wandering.

Know'st thou, a Saxon chief hath challenged me?

*Eth.* No, not till now : what reputation has he?

*Osr.* 'Tis young lord Edwin, son of Ethelwulf,

From whom I took this castle.

*Eth.*                    Why delays

Sir Esmund from his duty?    But to speak

Of war was once to arm him ; e'en so swift

His sword flew to his thigh, his helm was on.

'Tis not his custom to be so remiss.

 *Osr.* O Cupid! is the story still to tell?

Girl, girl, where are thine eyes?  Alas! he chose

Thy silly self for his divinity;

And thou disdain'st him in the usual way

Of worshipp'd maidens.

  *Eth.*      He has left you then.

 *Osr.* Why, wouldst thou have him languish in thine

  eye?

 *Eth.* And therefore you are arm'd, and these poor limbs

Are lock'd in bitter steel?

 *Osr.*      No more of this.

Sweet Ethel, to thy chamber.

 *Eth.*      Oh, that e'er

So weak and trivial a thing as I

Should sever two such spirits, one my sire,

The other not being less than noble Esmund!

Forgive me, sir, for I am much to blame;

Yet pardon me, because I am a maid,

Whose privilege it is to be twice wooed.

Let him desire me in my humbler mood,

And I'll be changed.

  *Osr.*     Thou heart without compare !

Angel of mine, my dearest Ethelburga ;

Not while my lips have any breath at all !

What, pretty fool, would'st thou deceive thy father,

These silent martyrs in thy face the while ?

  *Eth.* How, sir ?

  *Osr.*    Thine eyes are witnesses against thee

Of violence intended to thy heart,

Which therefore in her windows sets these tears,

Like melancholy peeping prisoners,

To tell the world of cruel wrongs within.

  *Eth.* You are mistaken.

  *Osr.*    Nay, not I, my child :

Think'st thou to 'scape a father's watchful eye ?

But come, cease weeping, and shine forth on me :

Unfreeze my frosty vigour with thy smile.

Ah ! thou'lt dissolve me, if I linger more.

Go, sweet, and in thy chamber cloister thee

From the rude clamours of shrill-sounding war.

Thy pure soul, having privilege of heav'n,

Thither I'll send thee, my ambassador,

To beg a ghostly legion to my aid.—

Old man, I had o'erlook'd thee ; thou seem'st feeble.

[*To* EDWIN.

*Edw.*  I'll be your henchman, porter, scullion,
  groom ;

Hew wood, draw water ; let me sweep your halls,

Only to live with you.

*Osr.*          Fear not for that ;

I love thee, for the love thou show'st to me.

But be not vex'd, if I require thee not

To follow me afield : thou seest my daughter ;

Thy present service is to tend on her :

I charge thee, love her heartily.

*Edw.*            My soul

Be forfeit, if I do not.

*Osr.*                    Then farewell.—

Come, soldiers all, attend me to the field.

[*Exeunt* OSRIC *and retainers.*

*Eth.* Let me read o'er the volume of my heart :

[*Aside.*

Now on the first leaf is Sir Esmund writ :

Ah ! many a virtue is summ'd in his name ;

His valour, prudence, skill, shine forth in gold :

He loves me too ;—oh ! but he loves me deeply ;

Am I a woman, and not answer that ?

*Edw.* Hear me, sweet lady.

*Eth.*                    Can I see my sire,   [*Aside.*

To whom my life is all in duty owed,

So brave, so feeble, so necessitous,

His white locks so with glory shone upon,

Totter all ruinously, and know that I

From 'twixt his fingers have pluck'd forth the staff

On which his life leant ?   Shame, to stay so long !

I'll close my heart's book and peruse no further,

Content to wed Sir Esmund.

*Edw.*                    Madam, hear me.

*Eth.* Begone, begone, thou troublest me.—I'll read

[*Aside.*

No further in my heart, lest I meet that

Shall start me from my purpose, and cast loose

Me miserable.   Ah, this love! this love!

That, like a cross wind in my soul uprising,

Blows ope the second page.   Who was this stranger?

Go to, false framing lips, to call him strange

Who dwells in my heart's heart!   What word was

    that!

Yet whosoe'er he was, one thing is plain,

That duty for his sake seems like a Gorgon;

Turns me to very stone to think upon it.

But, O dear youth, I do devoutly pray,

Thou hast not done my heart that injury

To lightly speak thy love.

*Edw.*                    No, on my soul!

*Eth.* How know'st thou that?

*Edw.*                    I am his friend.

*Eth.*                              Whose, then ?

Didst thou o'erhear me ?   Man, how dar'st thou come,

And creep into my secret counsels thus ?

Begone, thou rev'rend subtlety !—His friend ?

But art thou now in very truth his friend ?

    *Edw.* Ay, madam, I might say we were one flesh.

    *Eth.* Tell me some news of him ; but first, his

        name :

Is he not noble ?   As men speak, I mean ;

For that nobility which nature makes,

His patent 's on his brow.

    *Edw.*              And dost thou love him ?

    *Eth.* My heart were void of joy, could I say no ;

Yet to my sorrow must I answer, yea.

    *Edw.* These sorrows, that do usher in sweet love,

Are like the clouds and wat'ry mists that hang

Upon the bright cheek of a summer morn :

But when the hours bring forth the blessed Sun,

Through all this weeping, sad, funereal host

He darts the splendour of his midday beam,

As enemies to his glad sov'reign state ;

Which soon being melted and dispersed to nought,

Then all goes happy, fair, and tranquilly.

*Eth.* At least, I thank thee for thy prophecy.

But thou delay'st to give me news of him

Whose sight shall gild my sorrow.

*Edw.*                    First, thine hand :

He hath no older friend than I myself ;

This kiss is for his sake.

*Eth.*               Hark ! some one comes.

Step hither with me, and say what thou know'st.


*Enter* ESMUND *and* HOSKOLD.

*Hos.* Look, yonder stands the man of whom I spoke :

See, how securely the bold traitor smiles,

Engaging with my lady : look you now,

He takes her hand.

*Esm.*              'Tis strange, she lets him do it.

*Hos.* Kisses it, by St. Peter !

*Esm.*                    So he does ;

And she, whom I accounted Virtue's self

(For so she is to me), chides him as one

Who rather chid the manner than the fault,

Because 'twas not committed on her lips.—

Go, fetch a guard.—That fellow told me right :

[*Exit* Hoskold.

'Tis like, this man is the young Saxon chief.

Soul of my fathers ! can it be he loves her ?

But what imports that now he's in my pow'r ?

Transparent youth, how he shines through 's disguise !

Can eighty years tread o'er the earth so light ?

To hands press lips of fire, with murmurs breathed

Upon the burning wings of deep-drawn sighs ?—


*Enter* Hoskold *and retainers.*

Release my lady's hand, thou counterfeit !

But for her presence, I would strike thee dead.

 *Eth.*   Sir Esmund, I'll not stay to quarrel with

  thee.

This ancient man had from my father charge

To tend on me : see, thou oppose him not.

Come with me to my chamber, good old man.      [*Exit.*

*Esm.* Stay yet awhile.                          [*To* EDWIN.

*Edw.*                    Why wilt thou hinder me ?

*Esm.* To tell thee that I know thee for a spy.—

Arrest him, fellows : 'tis the Saxon chief.

*Edw.* Am I discover'd ?   God and my lady, then !

*Esm.* Lord Edwin, thou but runn'st upon thy death :

Yield up thy sword to me, and thou shalt live.

*Edw.* To fight such odds were folly; here's my sword:

Heav'n and mine own just cause fight for me now !

*Esm.* Go, fellows, bear him quickly to a cell ;

On peril of your lives if he escape.

[*Exeunt retainers with* EDWIN.

Upon his finger shines a jewell'd ring ;    [*To* HOSKOLD.

Possess it while he sleeps, and bring it me.

[*Exit* HOSKOLD.

Since honourable means have fail'd their end,

I will seek out this chief's bereavèd men :

They, doubting not the voucher of this ring,

Will gladly to his rescue follow me :

Thus shall I win the castle.    But meanwhile

With certain desp'rate rovers will I treat

To ship Lord Edwin o'er the distant seas.

Most like his men (as sheep left shepherdless

Betake them to the wolf for government)

Will choose myself to be their general.

Thus shall this castle and its gem be mine :

Upon the guilty deed kind fortune shine !                [*Exit.*

# ACT III.

## SCENE I.—THE FOREST.

*Enter* HUBERT, OSWITH, THEODORE, *and others.*

*Hub.* Nay, sit thee down: why, boy; why, merry
    romp,
What's come to thee ?   A song, sweet child! a song !
*The.* No ; I'll not sing.
*Hub.*                    But if thou knew how I
Am musically bent this afternoon !
*The.* 'Tis not your wont; for when I sing to you
My prettiest airs, you talk, or make a noise,
Or move away, while I am singing best.
*Hub.* Oh, then I was not so inclined as now :
All pleasures have their season ; those we most ,

Affect, not being desired at present time,

Fall coldly on our spirits : who can brook

A merry tale, being busy, sick, or sad ?

Dainties delight us not when we are full ;

So sweetest sounds fall flat upon our ears,

That chime not with the passions of our souls :

But now mine inmost spirit is athirst

To drain the pleasures of sweet harmony.

 *The.* I do not care for that ; I will not sing.

 *Osw.* Will you not sit by me, boy ?   Watch me now ;

I'm making arrows of the yew-tree wood :

See, how I shape them smooth and taperly ;

Head them with steel, and feather them so swift,

They'll overtake an eagle.

 *The.*      'Tis all one :

I've seen you do 't before.

 *Osw.*     Not with this knife :

This pretty knife is quite unknown to thee.

 *The.* I'll look at that : who made it ?

 *Osw.*       I myself

Carved out the handle from a huge stag's horn :

The blade was temper'd by old Thor, our smith :

The handle's wrinkled like cook Frigga's face ;

The blade is sharper than her nose.

    *The.*                       Ha ! ha !

I love you when you say such funny things.

    *Osw.* Why, sit thee down, and eat thy supper then.

    *The.* No ; now I've seen the knife, I'll run away :

Maybe, Lord Edwin will return to night :

I'll climb the hill once more, and look for him.    [*Exit.*

    *Osw.* What ho, lad, stay !

    *Hub.*                Thou'dst better let him

    run.

Since my Lord Edwin to the castle went,

A prowling spirit has possessed the lad :

He is as restless as a little bird

That's wander'd from its nest : he will not eat ;

But frets about the forest all the day ;

While sorrow is so gather'd in his eyes,

Needs but another drop to swell it o'er.

*Osw.* He's right; 'tis strange, Lord Edwin comes not
   back.

*Hub.* I greatly fear, some mischief has befall'n.

Hark! some one comes this way :—Ho! who goes
   there ?

### *Enter* ESMUND.

*Esm.* A friend of the Lord Edwin's.

*Hub.*                        Oh, most welcome !

What news bring you of him ?

*Esm.*                        Art thou the man

Who, in his absence bears authority ?

### *Enter* THEODORE.

*The.* Just now one came this way.  Oh ! there he

   stands :                                [*Aside.*

His back 's to me ; but now he turns himself.

O holy mother ! 'tis the wicked squire :

That villain has dealt fouly with my lord ;

But if he's still alive, I'll seek him out.      [*Exit.*

8

*Esm.* I have a message to you from your lord;

But, doubtless, first you'd hear some news of him.

*Osw.* Ay, that's the main; first tell us, how he fares.

*Esm.* Unlucky are the lips that teach the crimes

Of Fortune wreak'd on spirits of great worth.

Would that another man of sterner mould,

Whose heart choked not the passage of sad truth

Might paint my dearest friend in misery!

Briefly, the worst; your lord in prison lies.

Ye know, beneath what weight of aged snows

Your lord had cover'd up his youthful fire;

And how his honour and proud chivalry

Lay hidden in the base weeds of a Dane:

E'en thus he enter'd in Lord Osric's castle,

Who, like a courteous knight and gentleman,

Shot forth kind welcome on his suppliant.

By chance a knave was idling in the hall,

A shrewd, suspicious, snarling, saucy knave,

Who, coming near Lord Edwin viewed him close;

Till, spying on his finger this rich ring,

With lifted voice, *Ho, ho, thou knave!* cries he,   ·

*Is this the badge of thy great poverty?*

*Where got'st it, thief?*   Whereat Lord Edwin's soul,

Through his poor habit flashing, gave him forth.

*Hub.* O, who, by putting on a sordid dress,

Can hide the spark of proud nobility ?

What garb can Brutus teach to play the slave ?

Ah, my dear master ! it has come to this

Because thou sett'st at naught old Hubert's love,

Calling him "preacher" with thy fiery lip

For moving thee to quit this rash design :

Oh, thou hast slain thyself!

*Esm.*                        Forthwith Lord Osric

Bade seize him, who resisted not, where no

Resistance had availed ; and so he was

Cast fetter'd into prison.

*Osw.*                    Tell us, sir,

How came you to befriend him ?

*Esm.*                        Thither I,

Proceeding secretly, conferr'd with him.

He, of my love being satisfied (it sprung

From certain jars betwixt my lord and me),

We thus compounded ;—To Lord Edwin's men,

Making but threat of arms, my influence

Should ope the castle gates, and (life apart,

Which to be spared) his should be all the spoil :

Upon which consummation, he should yield me

Lord Osric's daughter, to become my bride :

These terms consider'd, he consented to,

And wing'd me with this message hitherward,

Adding this ring for further testimony ;—

Look at it; 'tis your lord's.

    *Hub.*               I know it well.

You have but to command, and we'll obey.

    *Esm.* Why then, by all the love ye bear your lord,

And by the oath that ye have sworn to him,

Who now in darkness lies and fetters sharp,

Hung o'er, alas ! by cruel threat of death ;

Betake ye to your weapons, seize your bows,

Swords, battle-axes, pikes, or what ye have,

And set yourselves in my obedience,

For we'll attack the castle instantly.

*Hub.* Oswith, go thou that way, and sound thy horn :

I, on this side, will call our comrades to.—

In half an hour we will be all met here.        *Exeunt.*

———◆———

## SCENE II.—A PRISON.

*Enter* EDWIN.

*Edw.* If, to have come within the reach of joy,

To have talk'd familiarly and sweetly with it,

Have held it by the hand, and kissed it too,

Can, by comparison, arm present grief

With pang more keen and bitter to be borne,

Then am I truly to be pitied.

I had esteem'd myself more of a man

Than to be so moved by adversity :

I have forewarn'd my breast of troubles oft ;

Proposed griefs to my fancy ; taught my heart .

To anticipate the loss of what it loved,

As friends, life, liberty ; and thought by this,

Being so admonish'd, when misfortune came,

'Twould find me adamant : but now I see

The seeming steel of this philosophy

Pierc'd by the rude thrust of an accident ;

And myself, naked of all comfort, left

To the bleak pelting of the pitiless storm :

For, with what forethought we encase ourselves,

There's still some chink unthought on ; through the which

Misfortune creeps, and the defence is lost :

Nor can our sum of miseries be cast

Until experienc'd home, more just than he,

Who, standing on the comfortable shore,

Can tremble with the tossing mariner.

I have lived not unhappily ; yet deemed,

At any time, I could have look'd on death

With an indiff'rent, dry, and sated eye,

Nor held the grave more fearful than my bed,

Until one day made life a blessed thing,

And the next brought my doom.   O God! O God!

Thus to be snatch'd away so suddenly,

When life was fairest, and Hope at her noon

Made of this usual earth a festival

And paradise of sweets, where'er I turn'd!

E'en in the sunny hour of maiden love,

And when my heart, swoll'n high with too much bliss,

O'erflow'd this common world of things, that all

I touch'd, or tasted, heard or look'd upon,

Seem'd fraught with a new pleasure!   O, 'twas hard!—

But to my pray'rs again!   I have sinn'd much ;

Yet haply He, who judg'd me, may repent,

As once He did for erring David's sake :

Though let me, for my safety, take good heed,

I mock Him not with service of my lips.


*Enter two Rovers.*

Who's there ?   What are ye, who thus darkly break

Upon my meditations ?

1*st* *Rover*.          Hist, no noise !

Speeches are cutthroats : not a word, sir thane !

We come to take you hence.

   *Edw*.          Ha ! whither would ye ?

  1*st* *Rov*. You'll know more certainly when you are

      there.

  *Edw*. I will not go with ye until I know.

  1*st* *Rov*. Pinchcheek, thou hast the cord ; go, bind

      the lord.

  2*nd* *Rov*. Is he a lord ?   The devil from his eye

Hangs a most ugly sign.

  1*st* *Rov*.          Pinchcheek, thou'rt sober :

I will report thee sober to our chief.

Where is thy valour, sir ?

  2*nd* *Rov*.          Thou hadst it last.

  1*st* *Rov*. In verity, here 'tis, in my left pocket.

Drink ! drink !

  2*nd* *Rov*.     Now, thane ; I fear thee not, not I :

Here goes to bind thee, thane.

  *Edw*.          My death's resolv'd on ;

And, by the God I serve ! I will die here :

I will not budge an inch.

  *2nd Rov.*    He will not budge.

  *1st Rov.* Pinchcheck, another dram ! this time for

   wisdom,

Because thou giv'st despair so little line.

The thane talks nature : who can root his feet

With willing heart out of his native land ?

Haply our children, climbing on our knee,

Have found the windows of our bosoms ope,

And, pretty fools ! crept in, and nestled there.

Or else our sad wife, standing on the shore,

With kerchief at her dim o'erflowing eye,

Weeping and waving at moist intervals,

Is like a sight of death to look upon.

Or else we leave a maid, our sweet first love,

Our own peculiar and heart-doting treasure ;

With many a kiss sealing her constancy,

And oaths to double-lock her plighted troth,

So sail we forth upon the boundless sea ;

Beyond the blue horizon stretch we on :

But when we come again, when we return,

I say, when we come back :—what talked I of ?

Pinchcheek, the thread !

> 2nd *Rov.*          The cord ? here 'tis.

> 1st *Rov.*                                    Fool ! fool !
>
> I ask'd thee for the thread of my discourse.

> *Edw.* Thou foolish drunken fellow, what's thy name ?

> 1st *Rov.* Drawcork, an 't please you, sir: was butler
>
> once
>
> To a monast'ry, and learn'd my letters there.
>
> O, I can talk :—Pinchcheek, be evidence.

> 2nd *Rov.* Yea, thou'rt the opiate of the elements ;
>
> I've seen the stormy wave, when thou harang'st,
>
> Hang down his crested head, o'ercome with sleep,
>
> And low'r it on his placid heaving bosom.

> *Edw.* Away ! out of my cell ! ye trouble me.

> 1st *Rov.* Why then, come quietly.

> *Edw.*                          I will not go.

> 1st *Rov.* O, what a sweet simplicity is this,

When mortals kick at sheer necessity!

Thou, to that arm, Pinchcheek; I'll carry this.

   *Edw.* Let him attempt me, who's in love with death.

Weak knaves, ye weary me! out! get ye gone!

                            [*Driving them out.*

   1st *Rov.* Run, Pinchcheek, to the shore, and bring

     more aid.                    [*Exeunt rovers.*

   *Edw.* And yet, I do repent me to have fought

So hard against the swift sure hand of Fate.

Am I a Hercules to laugh at armies?

Or god, akin to the dire elements,

That, single-handed, thus I dare my foes.

'Tis said, the anticipation of an ill

Is th' ill itself; nor has death any pang

But what we make ourselves by thinking on it:

Ay, could we lift our thoughts beyond this life,

And hold for nought the idols of our hearts!

So, as I am a Christian, let me do it,

And purge my heart of earth :—farewell for ever,

Thou sweet delusion; thou dear vanity!

Thou momentary dream so fraught with bliss,

That, hov'ring but upon the verge of slumber,

Scarce show'd thyself most fair, and thou wast fled !

Fair flow'r of earthly hope, born but to die,

Fall'n on a soil so all unfortunate !          [*A lute outside.*

Is this an angel, come to sing my dirge ?

 *The.* (*sings outside*)—

> A pilgrim stood within the hall,
>     And spake this trembling word,—
> " O Lady Margaret, I bring
>     Some tidings from thy lord."
>
> " And is he well ? " in haste she cried ;
>     " O wilt thou never speak ? "—
> " Ay, well ; though many a tale of woe
>     Is writ upon his cheek."
>
> " And shall I soon behold my lord ? "
>     Her breath she quickly drew ;
> For, from within the stranger's hood
>     A stifled sob came through.
>
> She gazed : he turn'd the hood : she saw
>     Lord Stephen's noble crest ;
> And swoon'd, and without motion lay
>     Upon her warrior's breast.

*Edw.* It is my Theodore, my prettiest Greek !

O thou disposer of all good, hast thou,

To warn me of thy near advancing grace,

Sent on thy smallest angel from the sky ?—

Hist, Theodore !—Sweet boy, he cannot hear me ;

The casement is so small, and set so high.

O, for some means, to teach him where I am !

See, here's a tile that's fallen from the roof ;

My dagger's point shall be my pen for once :-

" *Between the castle and the neighb'ring shore*

" *Post, with all speed, a dozen men at arms.*"—

My heart with thee, thou speechless messenger !

Thou bear'st Lord Edwin's fortunes in thy flight.-

The boy has pick'd it up ; he waves his hand,

And kisses it to me :—run for thy life,

Thou pretty ling'ring fool !—I think he hears me ;

So swiftly o'er the ground his light feet fly.

Hark ! I hear steps along the corridor :

I will do what I may to draw out time.

## SCENE III.—A ROOM IN THE CASTLE.

*Enter* OSRIC *and* ERIC.

*Osr.* Tell o'er thy news again ; my soul abjures it :
Esmund, a traitor !

*Eric.*                Ay, within this hour
The scouts predict him here.   Bear up, my lord ;
You take this news too heavily.

*Osr.*                    O Esmund !
I loved thee, Esmund ! rear'd my hopes on thee,
Leaned my infirmities upon thine arm,
Trusted thee with mine honour.   Let the staff
Henceforth cast off its owner, and the ground
Under the superstructure yawn its grave.
Ungrateful man ! thou eat'st at mine own table ;
What secret of my heart held I from thee ?
Or what possession thou might'st not have shared,
So near my bosom ?   I am an old man ;
And my last words must be, all men are liars.

Heav'n pardon thee for this, thou cruel man,

To have deceived me so !

  *Eric.*               We should not grieve

As though no man had suffer'd pain before ;

Or think, because we grieve, our fates draw on

Some solitary special-pointed curse.

Sorrow is such true link 'twixt man and man,

That oft we comfort and much solace draw,

By the remembrance of another's woe.

How many noble spirits, ere your own,

Pierc'd by the sharp point of ingratitude,

Have felt how deeply those they love can sting.

  *Osr.* Go, go ; I cannot reason with my grief ;

Could I but do so, I'd no grief at all.

When I'm in pain, what comfort is 't to think,

That Cæsar suffer'd too ?    What's he to me ?

Each heart 's a sep'rate world ; and feels no more

Another's grief than parallels can meet :

To think on Cæsar's pain, soothes me as much

As Cæsar consolation drew from mine.

*Eric.* Well, here comes comfort of another kind ;
And so I'll leave you, to collect some news.        [*Exit.*

*Enter* ETHELBURGA.

*Osr.* O my supreme of cares ! God shield thee, child,
With stouter arm than mine !

*Eth.*                        You call'd me, sir :
What would you with me ? but the tale that has
So drear a frontispiece, must needs be sad.

*Osr.* Ay, Ethelburga, thou must read with me
The book of sorrow.   Ah ! my gentle girl,
When I did teach thee first thine alphabet,
How testy and how wayward didst thou seem,
Fighting at each step of my patient love :
How oft the tedious book was flung away
Blotted with tears, and torn with angry fingers ;
Thyself as sulky and as full of woe
As if the griefs of Niobe were thine :
With pictures would I win thee back again
To slip instruction through thy pleasèd eye ;

And thus I wooed thee to the sweets of knowledge.

E'en such a childish and a fancied ill

Was bitter to thee, for thou wast a child ;

But now, to meet thy riper-judging eye,

Another volume is most sternly set,

Whose dark realities no art can charm,

Nor kindliest tutor to thy taste commend,—

The sorrows and mishaps of human life.

*Eth.* Ah, sir ! give me the book ; thou'rt old to teach ;

And I will be instructor in my turn :

Do thou but count thy sorrows out to me ;

And, for each sev'ral one, it shall go hard,

But I will match it with some comfort still.

*Osr.* First, Esmund is a traitor ; fall'n away,

And leaguèd with my foes : in him all men

Seem perjur'd, for I held no man as him.

*Eth.* Ah ! friends are still our shrewdest enemies ;

The shaft that strikes us from the hand we love,

Doth rankle in that sacred inmost part

Not all the malice of our foes can reach,

And wound us beyond healing.   Oh, 'tis pity

That nature, who frames heroes, yet should leave

Their tend'rest part unarm'd !   My words were boasts,

That promised comfort for an unknown ill :

Alas ! I have no balm for such a wound,

Unless it be this kiss.

    *Osr.*               The best of cures !

Bruised heart no other salve than love endures.—

But come, my angel, thou must put from thee

The woman; in an hour the traitor's here :

Heav'n guard thee then from his polluted hand !

    *Eth.* Thou wrong'st me but to waste a fear that way.

Virtue is virtue's safeguard ; many a queen,

Wanting that last defence, in peril stands,

Though tower'd in a nation's heart of hearts

And awful with their swords.

    *Osr.*             Brave girl, 'tis pride

To have been thy father.

    *Eth.*          Is there no resource ?

What has befallen to your soldiery ?

*Osr.* My men-at-arms are rebels to the core :

Esmund did train them ; they are all his creatures.

I have experienc'd, that he, who sleeps

On his own interest, to ruin wakes.

E'en thus I found it, when I durst review

The men who call me, leader : mid the array

Mine eye did wander, and required still

Those old companions of my chivalry,

Those pillars of my heart, my noble Sweyn,

Brave Edric, and his brother Ethelward,

Knute, Harold, Leofric and Heroman ;

And finding not, whom Death had ta'en away,

But in their stead new forms and faces strange,

As chill as old Deacalion's stone-born brood,

I was enforc'd to turn aside, and weep.

 *Eth.* My comfort's dumb: but say, what happen'd then ?

 *Osr.* What then ?　Why, marry, that among these knaves,

Authority is grown a standing jest :

A chief, who, in my youth, was half a God,

Is now the whetstone for each boorish wit;

My person, arms, limbs, manner, motion, gait,

Yea, mine infirmities became their sport :

Saith one to 's neighbour, plucking him by th' arm,—

" *This is a wizard, come to fee the moon ;*"—

" *A priest by 's beard,*"—the second knave replies,

" *Where will he place him to command our march ?*"

" *Ship-fashion, at the stern,*" the fourth returns :—

Whereat being hotly moved, I drew my sword,

And smote one scoundrel to his native earth,

When instantly,—Oh, act incredible !—

As thick as startled wasps they rush'd at me,

Bound down mine arms, removed my sword away,

And mock'd mine indignation with the shout

Of my supplanter, worthless Esmund's name.

With difficulty I released myself.


*Enter* ERIC.


*Eric.* My lord, the traitor, Esmund is at hand,

With a strong force of Saxons after him :

Look not to be supported by your men,

For false as Judas is each sev'ral one.

*Osr.* Fly, Ethel, to thy chamber :—quick, my sword.

*Enter* ESMUND *and followers.*

*Esm.* Lord Osric, sheathe your weapon, and fear not ;

No thought of mine is levell'd at your life.

*Osr.* I do not thank thee for thy mercy, traitor ;

Thy thanks are rather due to these grey hairs,

If thou hast any mercy to bestow.

*Esm.* Sweet Ethelburga, I would speak with thee.

*Eth.* Too well thou know'st I cannot answer no.

*Esm.* Nay, lady, thou hast scorn'd me long enough :

Is this discreet, to frown and turn thy back,

Or, as thou dost now, through thy lifted eye

To show thy soul on fire with sparks of pride

At him whom Fortune has set o'er thy fate,

Yea, and the lives of those thou holdest dear ?

The haughty soul most suffers in the mire :

I should be sorry, to be forced to teach thee

The bitter lesson of humility.

Thou know'st, thyself hast forced me to this pass ;

Therefore do thou, without more siege of words,

Surrender, while my love's still courteous :

I could more roughly woo thee if I pleased,

Seeing thy person is my prisoner.

*Eth.* And of my better part thou hast her scorn.

*Esm.* Scorn is a weed that from neglect doth grow,

But love is the rich fruit of tender care.

Pray'rs are the gentle gales that quicken love,

And still 'tis nourish'd by fast-falling tears ;

Till, to the eye of the glad labourer,

Who smiles to look, it spreads its timid leaves,

And, 'neath his sunny welcome growing bold,

Doth round his bosom fast entwine itself :

Thus love is quicken'd, foster'd, cherish'd, rear'd.

So, Ethelburga, let me tend on thee ;

Since to obtain the treasure of thy love,

Shall still be all the business of my life.

*Eth.* Eternity shall but increase my hate.

*Esm.* Then must I use a rougher argument :—

Look, Ethelburga, that thy filial hand

Pluck not my vengeance down upon thy sire !

If the fierce tyranny of the icy north

But breathe upon the solitary leaf,

Thou know'st how soon it falleth to the ground ;

E'en in so frail a balance stands thy sire.

By Heav'n, I will not shrink from any lengths,

To conquer thy submission ; so reach forth

Thy hand, in witness thou wilt be my bride ;

Or else, by all divine, thou shalt bring down

Sorrows as thick as hail upon thy sire.

    *Osr.* Fellows, I will have leave. Hear, daughter,

        hear me :

If, to the siege of that abandon'd man,

Thou but unbarr'st thy silence of a term

That hints surrender :—if thou dost, I say,

But flatter him with one beseeching look ;

A father's pray'r shall post on wings to heav'n,

And sue a curse on thee and all thy line.

*Esm.* What, am I conqueror, and bearded thus ?—

To your duty, fellows ! go ; away with him :

Go, all of ye, and leave us for awhile.—

    [*Exeunt all, save* ESMUND *and* ETHELBURGA.

Think, Ethelburga, dost thou well in this ?

What, wilt thou be thy father's murderer ?

*Eth.* To heav'n I do commend myself and him,

E'en to that power that breaks the lion's teeth,

And from the mortal snake can pluck the sting.

In God I trust, who will deliver me,

And turn aside the aims of wicked men.—

Base man, thou hast no pow'r to injure me.

  *Esm.* Thou mak'st me mad, thou scornful girl, thou

   dost.

I am not further to be trifled with :

Look on thy lover, or Death looks on thee.

  *Eth.* Death be my choice, then, whom in sooth I love

Than guilty Esmund more.

  *Esm.*     Thyself hast put

The angel from my bosom, who till now

Hath been thy mute preserver :—enter, then,

Ye spirits of evil, and possess me quite ;

Inspire me, all ye devils ;—I am weary

Of gazing on thy beauty at arm's length :

A kiss, though it consume me !

*Eth.*                    Help, O heav'n !


*Enter* EDWIN, *and a few followers.*

*Edw.* Ruffian, let go !   Thou soul of treachery,

A second time hast thou deserved thy death,

And shalt thou live ?

*Esm.*            Lord Edwin !

*Edw.*                    That's my name :

I'll set my signature upon thy heart.

*Esm.* Art thou come hither in the flesh indeed ?

Or, but a spirit, to call me to account ?

*Edw.* Too long a story for hot blood !—die, traitor.

*Esm.* Lord Edwin, stay ; a moment, stay thine

  hand :

I own my life is richly forfeited ;

Yet to a dying man deny not shrift.

My soul doth wallow on the ground with guilt :

Oh, let me lighten it, ere I go hence,

And wash it with some tears of penitence.

    *Edw.* Short shrift, long cord would grace thine
        actions best.

    *Esm.* How thou cam'st hither to mine overthrow,

Against the fate I had contrived for thee,

The God of judgments knows, to pierce whose ways

Were vain.—I ask not this ;—besides my time

Is all too short to urge my penitence :—

Yet can it be, I am so swiftly fall'n

Who but a moment rode so royally

Upon the proud top of iniquity ?

O shame, thou art sin's shadow : e'en so close

Thou followest upon the guilty man,

Pursuing him with thine uplifted mace,

That ere the wretch hath time to say, I prosper,

Thy blow, descending on the godless boast,

Shatters his brittle greatness to the earth.

*Edw.* Continue in these thoughts, and thou'lt be wise ;

Thou hast already mended half thy fault.

*Esm.* First, shall my knee contritely sue for peace

From her to whom I did intend most wrong :—

Lady, sweet lady, pardon, if thou wilt,

The guilty aim of this wrong-seeking heart.

*Eth.* All I can pardon is remitted thee ;

And, for a free gift, thou shalt have my pray'rs,

To further thee with heav'n.

*Esm.*                          Sweet saint, how does

Thy goodness, like a fair and shining light,

Set off the depths of mine impurity !

Now could I wish to live, to learn to die.

*Edw.* Tell me, how thou wilt use thy liberty.

*Esm.* Not far from this a monastery stands,

That, from the reedy bosom of a fen

Uplifts its dark and solitary walls :

Croyland, its name ; for learning famed of old,

And od'rous memory of many a saint

Whose mortal bones enrich its sepulchres.

Thither will I, while yet the spring of life

Calls nature to rebellion in my blood ;

This martial vanity put from my side,

And all the pride and fiery lust of arms

Quench'd in the bosom of humility,

Retire with the sad burden of my guilt.

I'll change my name, that it shall be forgot,

And pass away, e'en as a leaf that's fall'n,

From the gay interchange of carnal men,

To be recorded in the book of life :

And thus, in sorrow, shall my years be told,

Till the sad tale have end.—All day, with pray'rs,

Strict meditations, and denying fasts,

Will I be instant upon Holiness ;

But when the eye of night shall gleam on me,

I will awake the fury of mine arm

To scourge the pride of this rebellious flesh,

That as a wall of sin parts me from God ;

Till mercy, peeping forth with piteous eye,

E'en from the bosom of the righteous Lamb,

Shall look upon my sincere penitence,

And drop moist quittance on my sin's account.

*Edw.* Happy is he who so o'ercomes the world

That he can count it dross ; but few there be,

So sweetly temper'd to celestial things,

And with that heav'nly, glorious armour dight,

That they can wage this war.  Far, far beyond

All human laurels is that wondrous man,

Who, spurning the vain crowns of earth, aspires

To war against the flesh and its desires.

*Esm.* Farewell, Lord Edwin : God hath fought for thee.

Thou hast a heav'n on earth in thy sweet bride.—

Reach forth thine hand, sweet lady, that my lips

May bid the world adieu upon 't.  Oh ! now

Farewell for ever to all earthly bliss ;

Pleasure hath passed away in this last kiss.  ⌞*Exit.*

*Edw.* Peace go with him, and comfort him in time !

I dare not for my conscience seek to win,

From holy mother church a proselyte :—

Forbid it, Heav'n !—but 'twas a noble mind

That should have flourish'd loftily, had not

The angry breathing of hell-heated passion

Swept o'er the buds of his ill-fated youth.—

Go, bring Lord Osric hither, some of you.

*Enter* OSRIC.

*Osr.* Young Saxon, of his own accord he greets thee ;

Thy foe, Lord Osric ; now, by fate of war,

Thy captive.   But my heart is comforted

A little, by the thought of thy brave father

Whose life I spared, and whom, with thee, his son,

I freed from bonds; more, by thy looks, wherein

Nature hath set no stamp of cruelty ;

But chiefly, by thine actions, which have saved

My girl from the lewd handling of a rebel :

All which assurances speak in me now,

When I beseech thee to restore my daughter,

That we may pass together from thy castle,

And live in virtue, if, perchance, to die

In poverty.

*Edw.*     What, am I favourite

Of Fortune to no end ?   Ah, dear my lord !

Is 't well, is 't right, to filch from victory

Its pith and kernel ?   Trust me, I'll not yield.

   *Osr.* My heart misjudg'd thee : welcome, then, the

      worst !

   *Edw.* The worst thou'rt welcome to, if thou mean this.

That I restore this castle back to thee ;

If this content thee, I've a giving mind.

I see suspicion crowd into thine eye :—

What, ho, my men ! attend to what I say :

Into Lord Osric's hands, I, with this ring,

Consign your duty and obedience.

   *All.* Lord Osric ! we desire no better chief.

   *Osr.* What means this riddle ?

   *Edw.*                       But for this choice part

Of Fortune's favour ; even for her who makes

All riches cheap ; this gift will I retain,

And with my life defend it.

   *Osr.*                  Dost thou love her ?—

What say'st thou, Ethelburga ?   Mute ?   Yet so

Looks not a maid when she would answer no.

   *Edw.* What, not a word ?   Oh, then thou lov'st me

      not.—

Am I a child again, that will not read

The characters my very soul doth know ?

O ecstasy, that dims mine eyes, to trace

All Cupid's volume writ in one sweet look !

   *Osr.* When I was young, I too could read that book.


         *Enter* THEODORE.

   *The.* A prodigy, my lord! a prodigy !

   *Edw.* What, Theodore? come hither, bird, to me :

Sure, heav'n ne'er pack'd an angel closer !   How

Shall I reward thee ?   Oh, no way but this,

My love shall wipe the debt out with a kiss.

   *The.* O, hadst thou seen his sides all white with

      foam,

His parch'd tongue lolling from his gory mouth,

That dewed the ground ; so stiff, so feeble too !

# EDWIN AND ETHELBURGA.

## ACT I.

### SCENE I.—THE FOREST.

*Enter* EDWIN *and* THEODORE.

*Edw.* Enough, sweet Theodore ; go, play, dear boy;
I'll hear thy music at a merrier time.

*The.* Why is Lord Edwin sad ?   The live-long day,
With leaden step has he paced to and fro,
Putting the merry forest out of tune.
Why have I seen him oft o'erslouch his brows ?
Then, while to pleasure him, the sweet birds sang
Under their green roofs, mid the summer leaves,

1

In misplaced melancholy sit alone,

And muse, and sigh, and cover up his face

Within his hands, until a tear stole through?

Why is Lord Edwin sad?

    *Edw.*                I cannot tell.

    *The.* Say rather, that you will not.

    *Edw.*                     Cease to inquire:

I am not sorrowful, if something sad.

Times are, 'tis sweeter to be sad than merry;

Say, this is so.

    *The.*       But is it sweet to weep?

Flows pleasure in salt tears?   Or all at once

Does melancholy seize upon the soul

Where never that dark humour dwelt before?

For, till we lately to this forest came,

I never saw you sad.

    *Edw.*         Well, well; thou'rt right:

This forest's sight has filled my soul with grief:

There rest thee, Theodore, and ask no more.

Thou canst not aid me with thy little strength

To do the business that I have in hand:

Nor would I stain thy young brow with my cares,

Because I love thee much, dear Theodore.

   *The.* O monstrous love ! to be so double-faced,

To pat my cheek, and wound me at the heart :

All sting, no honey ; like a cruel wasp !

Thou wrong'st me,—oh ! thou dost ; I say, thou dost ;

When, day by day, thy very eyes have seen

My strength grow to the level of my love.

Why dost thou love me, say ?

   *Edw.*                      Thou foolish boy !

Who can say why he loves ?   Thyself say how

Thou mak'st thyself belov'd.   Think, if you will,

My heart, debarr'd from other vent, so spends

Its soft and sentimental part on thee.

   *The.* Come, say what's forward.

   *Edw.*                  Willingly, I would ;

But that the tale might ruffle thee with fear.

   *The.* In twilight does each tree a ghost appear.

A secret's worst is in the worst way told,

When secrets in friends' faces friends behold :

For mystery sets Fancy on the wing,

To spy a bugbear in each mortal thing ;

Which, if 'twere seen with vision less alarm'd,

Were of its dreadful colours half disarm'd :

As many terrors as the breast appal,

Uncertainty is mother of them all.

    *Edw.* Thy love hath conquer'd : come, I'll tell thee all.

Sit closer, Theodore : put by thy lute.

    *The.* I'll hang it on this bough, to catch the wind,

That's full of love-sighs.—Oh, the silly wind !

'Twill measure out its sorrows by the hour,

And sometimes die outright of pure despair ;

But the next moment up it springs again,

And screams and raves with fury and mad rage.

    *Edw.* This England, as thou know'st, is my birth-land ;

Nor far from this, stands my ancestral right,

A castle hoar, whose high abutting front

Looks forth upon the deep ; here I was born.

Now, when I was a child less old than thou,

A most ferocious, bloody brood of men

Came sudden from the North.   Ere yet was time

To arm resistance, on our gates they pour'd,

Struck down half-rais'd defence, swarm'd in and in,

Rush'd through the chambers like the blast of doom,

And smote, and smote till stone walls rung with shrieks,

And under-whisper'd groans, muffled with blood.

My father,—canst recal him, Theodore ?

   *The.* Dim, through the vision of my childish days,

His aged face breaks sad and sorrowful.

   *Edw.* Oh, he had cause ; for while hard-press'd he

      fought,

My mother, then in second pregnancy,

Flew shrieking to his side ; yet, ere she reach'd him,

He saw her caught by th' hair and instantly

Brain'd by these devils.   In a distant room

I lay asleep, but suddenly I woke

And saw my father bending o'er my crib,

With armour all aflame, and fearful looks.

He caught me out, and strain'd me to his breast:

I hung about his neck, and scream'd for fright.

A blasphemous and blood-besmeared crew

Pursued him close : he laid me quickly down,

Caught up his axe, and sprang into the doorway.

Then I beheld him, (for it was a sight

To print remembrance on an infant's brain,)

Upon the threshold, root his firm left foot ;

His spacious chest unfold, that heav'd with fire :

Aloft he rais'd his arms, and in his eye

Defiance flam'd.

  *The.*   Strike with thy soldier, Heaven !

Descend upon thy cause, and show thyself.—

Oh, did he fall ?

  *Edw.*   No, boy, he did not fall :

For, as he stood thus firm, confronting Death

Who dark and closely overshadow'd him,

The leader of those men, a noble Dane,

Was fired with sympathy : he offer'd terms ;

And so, to save his child, my father stoop'd

To be a captive.

*The.*        What befell him next ?

*Edw.* To serve the sea-kings : but he grew belov'd

Of these rough spirits ; and of his brother slaves

So valiantly esteem'd, that, on occasion,

They, giving vent to their affections,.

Chose him their leader.

*The.*                    See, how inborn worth

Communicates itself : though overspread

With thickest smoke of fortune, it shines through,

And draws all knees to its confessed light.

*Edw.* For many years we roved the desert seas,

My sire, and I. and fifty valiant men,—

Fresh, jolly, lawless, appetitive hearts,

Chance-fed like the sea-eagles, and o'erroof'd

By blue ethereal Jove.    To do our wills,

In mere blind spirit of obedience,

They would have plunder'd heaven of her stars,

And snatch'd the silver moon from out the sky.

Ha ! ha ! when o'er the horizon peep'd our poles,

To mark the trader droop his fearful sail,

And creep into his hole!   The music faint,

The dancers shriek, coy maidens fly to th'arms

Of their spurn'd youths, who faster fled than they;

While like a furious and on-striding ghost,

The beacon flamed alarm from hill to hill.

   *The.* O Lord, the merry life o' the blue sea!

When shall I see't again?   Oh, when shall I

Be rock'd upon't once more?   Down, down to sink

Into the cavern of the awful deep,

And watch the wat'ry peril hang o'erhead,

Then, take the huge wave at his mighty spring,

And touch the stars! Anon, with sheet set fair

To the rough toying of the am'rous breeze,

Through the crest-tossing billow-ranks to ride,

Like Phœbus on his cloud-dividing steeds,

The mark of gods and men!   The music, heart!

The music of the hurly-burly sea,

When to our songs he roar'd his boist'rous bass,

And, as our jovial cups we clink'd, would come

Bolt at the vessel's side, and leap aboard!

Ho ! ho ! the fright that stain'd each cheek with death,

Or ever we came near : was not a fish

But thrust his bottle nose ten fathom deep,

And trembled in his cave.

 *Edw.* Peace, peace, thou little prating fool ! be still :

But I've a tale to make thee steadier.

Once, being set upon a Moorish barque,

We, in the teeth of a determin'd foe,

Forc'd bloody entrance.    All resistance slain,

Or bound, we search'd the ship ; and in the hold,

Found certain men, in chains ; most mis'rably

Pent up in darkness, filth, and pestilent air.

Among the rest, a pretty, pale Greek boy

Droop'd o'er his dying father.

 *The.*      Thine own hand

Undid the knotty bonds my father bore :

But when his limbs were free, methought I saw

His spirit come into his eyes, and smile ;

Then soar beyond his body, that grew pale

For very envy, that it could not follow.

*Edw.* In fine, for this thou know'st, my father died ;

And those who serv'd him with united voice

Swore to myself obedience.    For awhile

I sway'd these stormy hearts, these leashless wills,

Their head and demigod.    Yet in the breast

Of pleasure, mid all jovial circumstance,

Full oft the solitary thought would spring

That poisons joy.    'Twas for my native land

This sickness, that stole o'er my secret soul

Till it outgrew the use and habit of mirth,

And life wax'd tedious.    Finally I chose

From all my crew some fifty volunteers,

English kin-spirits, to my fortunes link'd,

And with a weary heart forswore the sea.

Now with my little band, yet strong in trust,

And thee, my Theodore, I stand once more

On mine own—homeless.    This same forest, where

Methinks the birds sing nought but dirges now,

Was once my theatre of throng'd delight.

Ah me! how mournful, dull, and leaden-cold,

Through each remember'd glade, the echo sounds
Of my strange manly feet! On this sweet bank,
O'erarch'd with massy leaves, my mother sate,
And watch'd me, as I play'd—Ah, memory!
There's not a tree, in all this wilderness,
But hath a voice, and hoarsely finds it out
To tell the story of departed days.
Upon the forest's verge my castle stands,
And frowns at me from its arm'd battlements.

*The.* Let cunning Fancy not beguile my lord,
Win it, and it shall smile, and turn about
Its armed teeth upon its present friends.
Why, what's a castle but the world in brief,
That dotes upon success and shelters it,
But at misfortune bristles virtuously?

*Edw.* True, boy, thy wit makes thee a senator.
Tickle sad sorrow with a merry jest
Until she smile. 'Tis folly, sure, to sit
With folded arms and sigh. Hence from my breast,
Vain grief! henceforth I'll feast my thoughts on war.

*The.* What is his name, the lord who holds your
    castle ?

*Edw.* Lord Osric, boy, if he be yet alive.

I have sent to him an ambassador

To crave a battle, that my cause may come

To Heav'n's arbitrament.—Look yonder, boy:

Are they not dress'd like Danes, who come this way ?

Let us stand out of sight.


        *Enter* ESMUND *with* HOSKOLD.


*Hos.* Oh, yet in pity hear me ! look, sir squire ;

My guilt's mine own,—all mine : t' expose it, were

To slay the innocence of my wife and babes,

Who with myself will be cast forth to die.

Consider it, sir squire, consider it :

How little is he wrong'd, who, being robb'd,

Can from his plenty not perceive the theft.

Our faults but testify that we are men ;

But he, who shutteth mercy from his breast,

Seems less than human.

*Esm.*                  Canst thou plead so fair,

Damn'd as thou art, in act ?    Ungrateful cur,

That bit thy master's hand !    Thou worse than

    beast :

Thou thing without a conscience, hear thy crime!

Naked, thou camest to our castle gates,

Thou, and thy wife, and shiv'ring little ones :

To pity moved by thy beseeching tale,

Thy tears, thy miseries, thy helplessness,

I drew thee from the cold, and housed thee warm :

I brought thee to my lord, who heard thee kindly ;

And, of his bounty, thou wert clothed and fed :

But when thy soul revived, and thou grew'st strong,

So warm'd the viper in thy guilty breast :

Unholy wretch ! thou didst purloin from him

Who gave thee life.

    *Hos.*                  It hath a golden tongue,

Temptation.

    *Esm.*              Gratitude, a heavenly one.

    *Hos.* My shame and penitence have struck me dumb.

*Esm.* And therefore will I overlook thy guilt :

Restore what thou hast taken, and my tongue

Shall not accuse thee to thy injur'd lord.

*Hos.* Most generous ! Oh, yet a second time

My saviour ! Thou hast touched me to the quick

By mercy. Oh, thou wrong'st the veriest thief

E'er swung on gallows, if thou thought his heart

Incapable of thanks ! This life thou'st saved,

I, from this hour devote to thee; henceforth

No charge of thine shall be so perilous,

Or grown so nigh to the pale edge of death,

But I will risk it for brave Esmund's sake.

Hast thou no present trust for me ?

    *Esm.*                  No, none.

    *Hos.* I'm sorry for it, since my zeal is hot.

Think o'er 't again.

    *Esm.*        Still none ; at least not now.

    *Hos.* More's in thy heart than speaks. Say, art thou

        crossed

In the bright path of thine ambition ?

His name!—and he o'ershadows thee no more:

Or stands some babe betwixt thyself and fortune ?

Him will I steal, and to the forest bear,

To find his nurse among the hungry wolves.

 *Esm.* Irresolution !   Oh, how oft have I     *Aside.*

In thought leagued with this villain : yet, all things

Falling miraculously to my wish,

And opportunity beseeching speech,

My tongue falls dumb.   O virtue ! is't thy voice

That chokes the guilty passage ?

 *Hos.*        Then, farewell :

I see, thou wilt not trust me.   Half thy tale

Blushes upon thy cheek : well, well ; how shame

Steals from a man all but the manly name.

 *Esm.* Fellow, thou growest rude.

 *Hos.*        My zeal did err,

And 'tis my zeal asks pardon.

 *Esm.*       I am harsh ;

Hoskold, forgive it me : thou may'st be false,

But well thou canst play honesty: I own,

Thy bluntness hath more oped my bosom, than

A speech of finer point.    Come hither, friend ;

I will confess so much : I am not happy.

    *Hos.* Marry, then use all means thou canst to be so.

    *Esm.* Man, as thou fear'st thy Sovereign above,

Wilt thou be secret of my confidence ?

    *Hos.* Sir Esmund, 'twas my love that swore e'en

      now

To serve thee : what avails to double oaths ?

Keep thine own counsel, if thou wilt mistrust me.

    *Esm.* Then listen, and I will unfold my grief :—

Lord Osric hath a daughter to his age,

Fair Ethelburga, whom I will not praise,

Lest I should slander a celestial saint.

Enough, I love her ; and, in her sweet quest,

Have wearied out a fruitless, misspent youth,

Which, else devoted, might have brought me to

Those shining goals of men, wealth and renown.

For she, or whether o'er my rank she soars,

Or that my person and rude soldier's tongue

Those graces lack that give affection wings,

Disdains the love that I do set on her.

Oft have I moved her, yet no favour won ;

To all entreaty is her heart love-proof ;

Till, when with grief and pain she sees me pale,

Her pity through her cloud of anger breaks,

And looks upon me with that rosy light

Might draw a damnèd spirit back to life.

Thus paradise hangs ever at my lip ;

Still, as I near it, flies ; still lures me on ;

And still my hope-enthralled feet pursue.

*Hos.* The miseries, sighs, lamentations, tears,

Sickness, and pains of heart, and weariness,

Griefs in all attitudes, and without name,

To make description weep to think upon,

That follow in the haggard train of love !

All Neptune hath distilled through lovers' eyes,

And from no other source derived his salt :

Old Boreas, who through the wood howls now,

Blew careless music from his jolly lungs,

Until his breath was tainted with love-sighs.

What man who in his bosom bears a heart,

And hath not proved a woman's subtlety ?

Look, when she smiles, she masks an inward storm :·

But when she would be gracious, oft she frowns.

Let wit be mute in woman's company,

And reason speak in sov'reign manliness.

Oh, sir, 'tis very much to be reproved,

That man, t'whose throne the great Creator link'd

Fair universal nature, should beseech

Favours that are his due : produce the rule,

And woman, in her turn, makes suit to apes,

Apes sue to fishes : yet, bore nature sway,

Woman in man should clearly recognize

Her prophet, priest, and king, and something more.

Look round, and glean experience with thine eye :—

Mark, how the fame of valour, show of strength,

A loud imperious tone, and lofty bearing,

Though wit be scant, draw woman's suffrages ;

Such man is pester'd and pursued by maids,

Till he abhor virginity ; while he,

Who, pale and silent, in the sunshine sits

Of the charm'd circle of his mistress' eye,

Winging his weary heart with true love-sighs,

And nightly nourishing his suit with tears,

For all requital hath his lady's scorn.

    *Esm.* Then, prythee, what wouldst thou enjoin me to ?

    *Hos.* To get her in thy pow'r,—to force thy suit.

    *Esm.* Peace, fellow ! lest thy words, profanely piercing

The sacred stillness of this leafy dell,

May breathe a voice in oaks, to strike thee dumb.

    *Hos.* Why, this it is, to give a saint advice :

Either be all for Heav'n, or not at all.

Take Virtue to thy heart, and shun thy love.

    *Esm.* It is a blessed thing, to sleep in peace.

    *Hos.* Sleep singly then, and envy not the man,

Who to his bosom shall entreat thy love.

    *Esm.* Ah, Hoskold ! there thou wound'st me verily.

Didst thou know how exceedingly I burn,

And am consumed, and tortured in this flame !

In sober truth, I am a man no more ;

Nor have a heart for anything on earth,

Save only to be mis'rable.

    *Hos.*                    Be happy.

    *Esm.* Then am I lost.

    *Hos.*                 Why, then, be virtuous.

    *Esm.* O God ! despair lies upon that side too.

I live in Hell, to earn my death in Heav'n,

And suffer for a promise, in the trial

And conflict of our souls, that then's most dark :

Ah, gamester, on what desp'rate die thou stak'st !—

Thine heart, thine all, upon a dubious gain !

Heaven ? 'tis in the bosom of my love :

Then Heav'n itself is Hell, if she's not there ;

And Hell with her were Heav'n enough for me.

My mind is toss'd about betwixt two seas ;

Fate, bring me then to anchor, how she please.

    *Hos.* Unhappy man, give o'er ; thou plagu'st thy-

        self :

What, be not thine own devil.  List to me :—

It is thy lady's wont each week to seek

A village, that beyond the forest lies.

 *Esm.* Ay, to o'ersee her father's tenantry.—

Oft have I seen my heart's sweet sovereign,

Encircled with her rustic worshippers,

Hearing their silly suits and grievances ;

Or, with the magic of her bright-beam'd eye,

Healing their quarrels ; e'en her presence hath

A harmony that quells contentious thoughts ;

Or alms-bestowing, with a grace so apt,

The tongue lies mute in the receiver's mouth,

Choked with the heart's commissions.

 *Hos.*        At day's close,

Through this same forest homeward she returns,

Thyself in company to guard her safe.

Now, here will I, with sundry men of trust,

Lie secretly in ambush ; and, when ye

Approach, rush out, and bear thy mistress off.

On Brackley moor, there stands a ruin'd house ;

Come thither to thy love, and urge thy suit.

*Esm.* Do, as thou wilt; but, prythee, say no more.

*Hos.* I'll to my fellows then: seek thou thy love:

All shall be ready, ere thou com'st with her.      [*Exit.*

*Esm.* Shades of mine ancestors, whose martial deeds

Blazed in the virtuous front of the noonday,

To the eternal shame of secret plots!—

Oh, gloriously enthroned o'er erring men!

Look not upon me now, lest reason sink

Beneath those holy, still, and quenchless fires:

Let me be coverèd with mine own sin,

That Heav'n hold me no more in memory.

Pure-thoughted girl! angel of innocence!

Two souls eclipse not with thy cruelty!

I would unlock desire with lawful key,

And save thee with a priest's chaste warranty:

But spurn my love, and sue thy friend in Heav'n;

In me thou'st none: yet to my pray'rs prove kind;

And I'll requite this wooing of hot youth

With an eternity of wedded truth.      [*Exit.*

*The.* A fox! a fox! Lord, wilt thou not give chase?

*Edw.* Run, Theodore, to Hubert, my chief man ;

And bid him through the forest wind his horn,

To call my men : I'll follow instantly.

*The.* Mark me ; I'm here, and now I'm gone.

                         [*Exit, running.*

*Edw.*                     Poor lamb !

The wolf hath come thee villanously near,

And, but thine heav'nly shepherd waked, thou'dst bled.

'Tis true thy father is mine enemy ;

But treachery is a disguised devil,

Who's foe alike to all.   I hear my horn

Startle the forest glades with echoing shrill :

I'll go, and with my presence urge despatch.      [*Exit.*

                —◆—

## SCENE II.—A VILLAGE.

*Enter* VILLAGERS, MUSICIANS, *&c.*

1*st* *Vill.* *(woman).* Now, by thine eye, thou lov'st me.

2*nd* *Vill.* *(man).*               Sweet, I do.

1st *Vill.* Ah, me ! how grew division 'twixt us

two ?

Say, did the treason through thine eye creep in ?

Or was't my scolding lips first sow'd the sin ?

Sweet love, the quarrel in thine eye began,

That corresponded with bold Marian ;

Though through the village 'tis for ever told,

She's ugly as a witch, and quite as old :

Ye had your signals——

   2nd *Vill.*                Dearest, say not this.

   1st *Vill.* Tell me, she's plain.

   2nd *Vill.*                Sweet, if you think,

   she is.

   1st *Vill.* Forgive me, then, if I did sulk and pout ;—

Who would not do it, being so put out ?—

And be more loving to me than of late.

   2nd *Vill.* I'll press my pardon on thy lips, my

   Kate.                          [*They retire.*

   3rd *Vill.* Since Heav'n was pleased to take away my

   wife,—

Not yet two months,—how barren seems this earth

Of every solace it was wont to have!

Sure none but fools would in this world know

    mirth,

When not a spot each treads on but may be

The laugher's grave.    Ye hills, whose nodding brows

Salute the morn, ye meadows and green vales,

I have no pleasure now to look upon ye,

For ye remind me that I once was happy.    [*He retires.*

    4*th* *Vill.* I will not be denied to look upon her.

    5*th* *Vill.* Well, well; I've warn'd thee to keep from

        her sight.

When Master Peter gave account of thee,

I saw her cheek inflame with sudden fire:

Thou'rt ruin'd if she look upon thee now.

Go, hide thee, till thy credit be repair'd.

    4*th* *Vill.* As moth to flame, or to the magnet,

        steel,

Or this gross earth to the celestial sun,

So am I drawn to her.           [*They retire.*

*Mus.*                  Look to your parts ;

My Lady Ethelburga comes this way.


*Enter* ETHELBURGA.


SONG.

Under a stately-tressèd tree,
   When quiet eve breathed sweet and holy,
A youth lay,—none so sad as he,
   That feed with melancholy ;—
      "My love's forsworn,
      Her vows hath torn ;
   Let me die, and quit life's folly."
*All.* Oh, let me die, and be forgot :
   What is life, where love is not ?


O'er the forest leaves she comes,
   Tripping with her little feet ;
On the grass she kneels her down,—
   "Art thou there, my sweet ?
      Do not chide ;
      For beside
   Thine, my heart doth truly beat."
*All.* Welcome, sweet sunny love, sweet April life,
   That lives at death of cold, rough Winter's strife.

All around her steals his arm,
   Tender light breaks through his frown,
On his bosom falls her head
   Gently, gently down.
      Wake, breezes ! flow
     In murmurs soft and low,
  And, wrapping round, love's faint sweet spirit drown.
*All.* Hush ! hark ! no sound : the moon sleeps still
  In valley, and o'er grass-clothed hill.


*Eth.* How moving is the voice of harmony

In silence breathed, under the fall of eve !

Methinks the night bends an attentive ear

And hither throngs more fast, while the faint stars

Show forth their tim'rous heads, to be resolved

What heav'nly creature 'tis that charms the air.

Friends, sing again, yet not so sadly now,—

A song that trips unto a merry tune.


### SONG.

  Who will be a forester,
    And in the greenwood dwell ;
  All day to chase the flying deer
  . Through copse and mossy dell ?

A yew-tree bow with arrows keen
   Upon his shoulder rattle ;
The spear gleams in his hand that shall
   Do with the chafed boar battle.

Ho ! holloa ! ho ! the deer bounds past ;
   His dog looks in his face ;—
Away ! away !—from far the blast
   Brings back the furious chase ;—

Till when at eve the western sun
   The em'rald trees doth tan ;
Back to his forest home comes he,
   A toilworn, hungry man.

Where Marian at her rose-twined door,
   In kirtle white dress'd neatly,
Him welcomes to her outspread store,
   And kisses sweetly, sweetly.

Who will be a forester,
   And in the greenwood dwell?
Who loves with me sweet liberty,
   This life shall suit him well.

*All.* Then hey ! hark, how my horn winds through the hollow !
   All ye who would pleasure, come follow me, follow !


*Eth.* Hath any man beheld Sir Esmund yet ?—

Sweet friends, my heart requites your melody

Beyond report of my untutor'd tongue.

*Mus.* We'll sing again.

*Eth.*                    I pray ye, sing no more.

Lest pleasure surfeit of sweet sounds, and die :

Too oft repeated sweets find wings, and fly.—

But see, the fire of slow-climbing eve

Is brightly kindled in the tall tree-tops,

To all pacific roamers on the wing

The signal for home-flitting.   If I stay

Much farther on the wrong side of this wood,

My fears will make me too a wingèd thing.

O Esmund, thou must needs be changeable

On a sudden, if thou canst be so remiss ;

But late thy fault was much the other way,

I could not rid my garment of thy pray'rs.

O God be thank'd ! he comes.


*Enter* ESMUND.


*Esm.* My love and service to your ladyship !

*Eth.* Thou comest late ; but that my fears forgive,

Because thou com'st at all.

*Esm.*                                    What ? angry, lady ?

Oh, chide me with a smile, if thou wilt chide.

*Eth.* Let us set forth.   Who is't, that weeps in black ?

[*To* 3*rd Vill.*

The best of men in tears, my sorrowing Maurice !

How shall I comfort thee ?   Alas, good man !

And yet, alas! my comfort is so small ;

Death has broke ope thy thrifty store of joy,

And stol'n thy treasure with his greedy hand.

We are all sport of that same cruel fiend :

But think, good Maurice ; think, thou woful man,

How short his triumph, and thine own, how vast,

When, through the dark and speechless vault of death,

The trump of resurrection shall sound ;

And thou, rising from sleep, shalt gaze on Christ,

Where, robed in awful majesty, He stands,

With many legions of bright-mailèd saints,

In the full hour of fated victory !

And when, from rank to rank, from choir to choir,

From height to height of the celestial throng,

The harps of seraphs shall advance his praise,

Till silence shall eschew itself and sing,—

Thou shalt behold, and meet, and to thee clasp

Thy risen, glorious, and transfigur'd wife,

To anchor on thy breast eternally.

Oh, think on this, thou woe-bewilder'd man,

And lift thyself above these clouds of care.

 *3rd Vill.* And so I will, and put my trust in Him,

Unto whose pity I commend my tears.

 *Eth.* Possessing hope, thou still enjoy'st thy lost one.—

Please you, Sir Esmund, that we now proceed.—

Oh, infamous! thou bold notorious man  [*To 4th Vill.*

That, wanting virtue, hast cast off the cloak

Of vice, mute shame, since thou has dared to meet me

In all the glaring newness of thy guilt.

What, thinkest thou thy character is dumb?

O villain! hath not guilt a tongue of fire

To brand itself in th' eyes of righteous men?

Thine actions, do they not proclaim thee, wretch?

Thy thefts, lusts, slanders, thy false-swearing lips?

Thy beastly and perpetual drunkenness ?

Thy words profane, that ope the wounds of Christ ?

Go, look upon thy fields, which thou neglect'st,

To sow this peaceful village o'er with broils.—

Answer me not, thou God-abandon'd man ;

With my reproof shall end thy tenancy :

Here thou abid'st no more.—I am too harsh ;

I see repentance swimming in thine eye,

And honesty, like the rich-laden bark

That o'er its limits swells the rising wave,

Float in upon that tide : I'll pause awhile.—

Farewell to all who love me.

> *Villagers.*            Blessings with you !

> *Esm.* Keep back, keep back, ye rude unmanner'd
>   clowns,

Out of my lady's path : ye are too forward.

> *Eth.* O shame, shame, shame ! Sir Esmund, cruel
>   man !

Wilt thou scorn love because its nature is

To rush in front of manners ?    Oh, to me

How fairer seems, and more to be desired

The rough, rude spirit of affection,

Though saucy, reckless, wild and turbulent

As th' ocean-foam that beats the doors of Heav'n,

Than thin profession lisp'd in choicest terms.—

Farewell again to all.                    *[Exeunt.*

---

## SCENE III.—THE FOREST.

*Enter* HOSKOLD *and another.*

*Hos.* What humours are in men! say, shall I laugh?

Or should it rather be a cause for tears,

To mark the ways of mad capricious love?

The dull grow witty, but the wise turn fools:

Those that were joyous once as summer flies,

Are mopers now to think upon their love,

Detest the world, forswear its company

But to be closeted with their sweet thoughts:

Yet see the man, t'whom not his bosom friend

Gave credit for the wealth of ten poor words,

As swift as fire talk down an orator

That would calumniate his mistress' chin.

I, the philosopher, am most the fool,

Because I love a man, who is in love,

And follow him as he his love pursues

For the reward of one approving look.

Yea, though the world beside accounts me villain,

Nor wrongs me much, for gallant Esmund's sake

Would I heap more damnation on my soul.

To see a man of noble qualities,

In counsels wise, in execution swift,

Brave, generous, of an exalted mind,

Grovel his greatness at a vain girl's feet

Who loves him not !   What maiden ever did

Requite the man who loved her most of all ?

I cannot teach my Esmund how to lisp

Or sing love's praises to the liquid lyre,

But I will show a royal road to woo.

The end of love is surely to win love,—

What matters then how won, if only won ?

Whether 'tis conquered or persuaded fair ?

Maids look not at the means when they're undone.—

Say, fellow, art thou perfect in thy part ?

Thou art ?   Stand back, then, till I signal thee.

                      *They retire.*

*Enter* ESMUND *and* ETHELBURGA.

*Esm.* Chide me no further, lady : a reproof

From those we love is as a volume spoken.

Like a stern wind around a ruin'd house,

Thou but reprov'st a heart that's desolate,

And empty of all joy.

*Eth.*               I'll say no more,

Unless it be with words to unsay my words,

And heal thee with that weapon caused thy wound.

I was too swift to judge a swift rash tongue :

Forgive me, if I grieved thee ; but thou didst—

Grant it, thou didst offend me grievously.

*Esm.* Jesu ! am I not mortal ? who could see,

That from his heart look'd forth, these ragged clowns

Cheering their faces in thy sun-bright eye,

And feel no envy ?

*Eth.*                    Thou dost grow too warm.

*Esm.* My heart's on fire, and shall my tongue be cool ?

Hast thou or heart to feel or eye to judge,

And rat'st me less in passion than the Finn

Whose spirit's bound in ice ?    I love thee, lady;

Yet have more strength than skill to tell thee so.

Oh, by whatever name shall I conjure thee ?

(For well thy beauty graces every name,)

My joy ! my grief ! my death ! my life ! my bane !

Why shunn'st thou Esmund, who would die for thee ?

Alas ! my person hath no shape of love ;

Nor is my tongue endued with happy skill

To tinkle sweetly in a lady's ear,

Yet this my merit,—that I love thee, lady.

When other men shall paint thee with their praise,

Count thy perfections with a ready tongue,

And I alone sit silent, cold and still,

This be my merit and redeeming grace,

That I adore thee more than all beside.

For loudest speakers but commend themselves,

Their heart still echoes back the flattery

Which they would heap on others : but true love,

When he would move a soul in trees or rocks

With the swift fire of his conscious speech,

Summons his spirits quickly to command,

Then like a vaunting general grows pale,

Falters, and dies in his own eloquence.

Be moved then, Ethelburga, with my suit,

At least for charity, and scorn not love,

Lest thou hereafter of scorn'd love be scorn'd.

*Eth.* Enough, no more : cease, and for ever cease.

Have I not told thee twenty thousand times,

I will not hear thy suit ?   I love thee not.

*Esm.* Thy reason, lady ?   Oh, declare my fault !

*Eth.* I have none other than a lady's reason ;

I love thee not, because I do not love thee,

Nor would a gentle mind solicit more.

Till late, I held thee in my best esteem ;

My sire,—nay I, and all—stand in thy debt,

For thou art valiant, active, skill'd and wise,

And gifted with the eye and spirit of rule,

By which, thou hast reform'd our warriors,—

A service beyond thanks in these fierce times,

When death flies o'er the sea on ev'ry wind.

To these opinions that I held of thee,

I credited thee with a soul of honour,

And should be loath to think I err'd therein :

Then, prythee, cease thy suit.—Thou seek'st my love,

And hast but barely 'scaped the plain reverse,

My scorn : thus in a heart that's wisely ruled,

Affection should be cured.

   *Esm.*               It lies too deep :

Contempt may cure a surface-shown desire,

But true love is enthroned beyond reproof.

   *Eth.* Thou feelest it, indeed.   Now, would my heart

Spoke not within me such a hopeless no !

Take comfort : fairer women are than I,

Milder in speech, and far more beautiful ;

And, from the ruins of thy present love,

Shall rise another of more auspices.

*Esm.* Oh, couldst thou know the inly fire of love,

How modestly it creeps into the heart,

And there, by secret, mute, and happy feeding,

Continually doth augment itself

Till reason have no pow'r to quench the flame,

Nay, rather joins her precious influence!

Alas! how wilt thou comfort my sick soul,

That dieth for thy love, thy love denied?

E'en as the leech, who with all drugs of earth

Encounters poison, save the antidote.

Grant me thy love, if thou wilt comfort me,

Which is more sweet and sov'reign to my soul,

Than cool redemption to a parched tongue.

*Eth.* I counsel thee, go from us for a season:

Time be thy nurse, whose light o'erpassing hand

Sows comfort and relief in ev'rything;

In darkness, day; sweet Summer's bounteous smile

Under the shaggy brow of Winter drear;

And, with the music of her rolling years,

Lulls sorrow into dim forgetfulness.

    *Esm.* If ever Time shall darken o'er this flame,

Which memory shall feed till my death's hour;

If e'er mine eye let slip a wanton look,

Or my heart sigh for other earthly thing,

Say, I ne'er lov'd thee : hold me for a jest,

A reed, a weathercock, and no true man.

    *Eth.* Though modesty should blush to see me so

Outstep a maiden's limit, still will I

Essay once more to be thy counsellor.

Waste not thy youth upon an idle chase ;

Quench not thy valour in the depths of love :

The boundless ocean hath more ports than one,

And he who from one haven is thrust back

To toss upon the weary boist'rous sea,

Doth wisely steer in search of peace elsewhere.

I counsel thee, go from us for a season :

Search out the world ; be look'd on ; air thy parts

Of honour in bright eyes and princely courts :

Ambition, be thy mark; I say, press on;

Set all thine heart thereto, and greatly win.

What, is't not more becoming to a man

To win bright glory from the gen'ral mouth,

Than to lie tangled in a lady's chain,

Pamp'ring his own despair?   Go forth, I say:

Free   breath,   for   fainting   sorrow!   Soon   thou'lt
        find

This variously shifting scene of life

Blow up the spark in thy pale drooping soul,

And ope thine eyes on new affections.

 Tis true, alas! thou art my father's staff,

His castle's rock, and, of his mut'nous men

Alone the forceful bond of unity,—

Still go, and Heav'n be with thee, as with us!

'Tis said, the harvest hath been plentiful

In the home-country, and the full-fed Danes

May haply give the world some breathing time:

There is no mention now of plunderers;

Seize th' opportunity.

*Esm.*               I will not go.

Thou know'st, I cannot live apart from thee.

But see, the night hath fall'n, while we have talk'd ;

And through the thin rear of yon drifting clouds

The stars peep wickedly.   Mischief's abroad

And couples with the wolf this fearful night.

How wild the wind amid the branches roars !

A storm frowns o'er the forest.   Thunder !   Hark !


*Enter* HOSKOLD *and another ;   the latter seizes*
ETHELBURGA.

*Eth.*  What  men  are  these ?    Help  me ;  help,
        Esmund, help !                                        '


*Enter* EDWIN *and Men.*

*Edw.* Am I too late ?   Fellow, release that lady :

What, wilt thou fight ?   Thy blood be on thyself.

                    [EDW. *fights the man, who falls.*

*Hos.* Fly, quick.                          [*To* ESMUND.

*Esm.*               Hast thou betray'd me ?

*Hos.*                                    No, by Heav'n!

*Esm.* I have a troop observing by the wood :

Let's steal away, and bring them to the rescue.

[Esm. *and* Hos. *steal away.*

*Edw.* Secure that man, and bring him to our

quarters.

Go, some of you, pursue the guilty squire :

My anger shall be hot, if he escape.      [*Exeunt Men.*

Now sweet thoughts to my heart, sweet utterance

Flow musically from my skilless tongue,

To cheer this pretty trembler : here she stands,

Her sweet pale face betwixt two lilies buried.

O God ! she needs must be most beautiful,

For beauty, like a daughter of the skies,

Ere she be seen, doth make her presence felt,

In trem'lous music o'er the spirit's chords.

Alas, would she but look upon me once !—

O heav'nly spirit of perfection,

Art thou descended upon earth ?   Bright soul !—

For grosser thing, I deem, thou canst not be,—

That art more beautiful than a saint's thought,

So holy, pure, and unexampled fair !

Oh, droop thy face no longer to the ground,

Lest the fond earth that roots the summer flow'r

Mistake thee for the pride of all her wreath,

And so embrace thee as her fairest child ;

But lift thine eyes, and sun those cheeks of snow,

Thou image of pale Dian, white with fear

And paler than the stilly midnight wave

Whereon the moonbeam trembles.   Does she hear me ?—

Rash man, I am her terror !   See, she lifts

Her eyes, and, meeting mine, droops them, as swift

As two faint stars that twinkle through the dark

And instantly retrieve themselves in night.

Sweet lady, let me do thee reverence.

    *Eth.* I'm in thy pow'r : I fear, thou'rt mocking me.
I pray thee, do not kill me.

    *Edw.*                    No, good sooth.

    *Eth.* For there are those will pay thee hand-
somely.

*Edw.* All worldly riches being summ'd in thee

Must beggar all thy kin. O lady, lady,

Since I have wrought some service for thy sake,

So let mine eyes some satisfaction take.

Wilt thou not look upon me once again ?

*Eth.* Was't thou came to my rescue ?

*Edw.* Ay, sweet maid,

From rude enforcement of unholy men.

*Eth.* I thought thou wert a robber.

*Edw.* In mine eyes

Are two fond thieves that would thine image steal,

To be the goddess of an empty shrine :

My heart hath long been desolate for thee.

*Eth.* I do not think I fear thee very much :

Methinks a robber should not look as thou :

Oh, if thy soul be of a piece with thee,

Stain not her beauty with a cruel deed :

Be gentle, for thy looks' sake.

*Edw.* By all the pow'rs that mortal faith o'ersee,

By thy dear self, which is the greater oath,—

*Eth.* What man was that,—O me!—what man
was he,

Who shamed my waist with his embracing arm ?

Oh, he did fright me, like a basilisk :

I would, I might forget his dreadful looks.

    *Edw.* He shall not live to frighten thee again.

    *Eth.* Nay, harm him not, I charge, or mine's the
pain.

But say, how cam'st thou hither, or what saint

Wafted thee from the farthest end of earth ?

    *Edw.* Heav'n, and pure breezes that eschew offence,

Did waft the plot into my timely ear ;

Forthwith I called my men, came quickly hither,

And thus thy rescue was accomplishèd.

    *Eth.* I thank thee from my heart.    Teach me thy
name,

That in my pray'rs I may remember it.

    *Edw.* Recall me by what name thou lovest best.

    *Eth.* Thine own were very well, if I knew that.

    *Edw.* Sweet, I am nameless, till thou christen me :

That name I bore, my heart hath put away

With an eternal, deeply-sworn divorce ;

For, I remember (oh, that this should be !)

That name was with thy race at enmity.

*Eth.* I'd rather that thou wert a robber now ;

Be one, that I may buy thy heart of thee,

With all the wealth I have.

*Edw.*                    Give me thy glove ;

I'll wear it in my helm ; and he, who wins it,

Shall wear my poor life too.


*Enter* THEODORE.

*The.* My lord, a troop comes riding like the wind,

Bristling with spears and shining o'er with steel :

In the firm front the crafty squire doth ride,

Beside himself with rage ; his frown of thunder

Makes answer to the lightnings of his sword,

With which he cuts the air.

*Edw.*                    Lady, dear lady,

Time has run out for love's sweet circumstance,

So, to the centre of 't: I love thee!   Dost thou hear?

And wilt thou understand me what I mean,

When I do simply tell thee that I love thee?

And wilt thou in thine heart think o'er my love?

And wilt thou put an ocean in that word,

Of oaths and vows, and think I pour'd it forth?    .

  *Eth.* I fear thy love's too sudden: for they say,

That true love grows not in a single day.

  *Edw.* I would there were an oath of that fine pow'r,

As would enforce belief by hearing it.

Might I but stay, I have such reasons—oh!

Such wealth of terms to gild my love withal,

Thou shouldst perceive it, like the sun in Heav'n:

But now 'twere death.   Hark! they are calling thee.

  *Esm.* My lady!                 [*Within.*

  *Edw.* Though I'm alone, I'll not relinquish thee

To that base man.

  *Eric.*         Ho! Lady Ethelburga!    [*Within.*

  *Eth.* 'Tis Eric's voice: my father's henchman calls.

  *Eric.* My lady!                 [*Within.*

*Edw.*          Sweet, farewell ; and think on me :

I will contrive some means to see thee soon ;

Oh, speedily I will.

*Eth.*          Farewell.          *Going.*

*Edw.*                    Farewell.

*Eth.* My soul returns, and wings me back to

    thee,                    *Returning.*

To say,—oh, yet I should not,—youth, though I

Know not thy name, my heart knows that I love thee :

Thou lov'st me too, thou say'st, and I believe thee,

Because to doubt, were pain.   Well, well ; thou dost :

Truth's in thine eye, and shall dispense with oaths.

    *Edw.* Yet let me register my true love's vow

Upon this tablet of fair ivory,

Which, if I forfeit, may I ne'er know bliss ;

And thus I seal my soul's oath with a kiss.

*Esm.* My lady !                    [*Within.*

*Eth.*          They're at hand.   No more, no

    more.                    [*Exit.*

*Edw.* It is my soul, that leaves me thus alone,

Then farewell, life ; end with my date of joy.

As one who, from a sweet and happy dream,

Far straying in some lonely ocean-isle,

Wakes suddenly to find his ship a speck

Fading far off at sea, and wrings his hands,

The while with careless, quick, distracted feet,

He treads the desert, sad, sea-beaten shore,

E'en so am I: now, solitude, I know thee,

Even to suffocation : I could weep.

 *The.* For sorrow ?

 *Edw.*     No, for joy : and yet not that ;

My joy 's away.   O Time, thou heart of ice !

Thou cruel, mute, slow, pleasure-quenching fiend,

Couldst thou not kill me in the interval

That thou hast interposed 'twixt life and life ?

But let me cast about to find some means

To gaze once more upon this paragon.

Be fav'rable, thou supreme God of hearts !

Thou babe of inspiration, shine in me

With all thy subtle, wise, discerning fire ;

Make me an angel of intelligence,

To plot the sweet encounter of my love.

Hist, Theodore !

  *The.*   What is it, my good lord ?

  *Edw.* Bring me the clothes of that hoar-headed Dane

Who died awhile since in our company.

Dost recollect him, boy ? He was a man

All white with age, and silver-bleach'd by Time.

His beard flow'd to his waist; beyond his feet

Jutted his wrinkled face, so crook'd he was :

With staff in 's palsy-shaken hands, he limp'd

Thus,—seest thou, boy ?—with such a crumbling step.

His looks would thrill all men with ghostly awe :

I've seen young warriors bow their steel-clad strength,

And give themselves to God, chanced they to light

Upon the creeping presence of that man.

Young Cupid shrive me for the sin, if I,

Who am a soldier listed in Love's wars,

Abuse my youth, to shut my warm blood up

In such an impotent receptacle.

There's more protection in a few gray hairs

Than in the steel proof of a coat of mail.

Thus mask'd, I'll enter in Lord Osric's castle,

And feast my soul upon this breathing pearl

That hangs in Danger's check.

    *The.*                     Oh, dear my lord,

Be not too rash.

    *Edw.*           Comfort, sweet Theodore !

For, pretty boy, when I have won my love,

I will prefer thee to become her page ;

That, in the sunshine of her glorious eye,

Thou may'st for ever bask.   But truce to words !

For the swift hours are but shod with lead,

Until my feet are wing'd towards my love.

# ACT II.

## SCENE I.

### A CHAMBER IN LORD OSRIC'S CASTLE.

*Enter* ESMUND.

*Esm.* Crosses that put some weaker from their
    ends,
Breed but new fires in me.   Still to pursue,
As mortals may, is to o'ercome ; so then
Fly on, ye swift desires ; on, burning thoughts !
As falcons, to o'ertake your beauteous prey :
My soul no longer shall restrain your flight.
Let me consider then.   That stranger, sure,
Whom some mischance thrust in 'twixt me and
    bliss,

Should be the wide-reputed Saxon chief

Of whose arrival in these woods I hear,

And rumour doth report he claims this castle.

'Tis well, 'tis happy, 'tis most fortunate ;

For my Lord Osric, being old and weak

And shatter'd with severe infirmities,

Hath for these many years devolved on me

All warlike matters.   Of his former troop

Few live that now remember him ; while I,

From time to time, have fill'd the gaps with men

Devoted all to me.   Then here's my plan :

First, will I break upon Lord Osric's sleep,

And rouse his numb age with the fearful sight

Of this same threat'ning Saxon ; on which vantage,

I will entreat him strongly for his daughter,

Who haply then may more submissive prove,

Out of pure pity for her helpless sire.

If not,—farewell to conscience !   I'll seek out

The Saxon, and propose my love shall be

The costly purchase of my treachery.                    [*Exit.*

## SCENE II.

### ANOTHER CHAMBER IN THE CASTLE.

*Enter* OSRIC *and* ERIC.

*Eric.* How fares my lord, to-day?

*Osr.*                        Why, Eric, well;

Better than old men use : thou know'st, my youth

Was not bestow'd on pleasure, therefore I

Do reap the fruits of honour in mine age.

*Eric.* And carry out the harvest bravely too :

Why, you should not be far off seventy?

*Osr.* But seventy?   Why, I remember me,

So many years back, for a boy of ten.

I'm eighty, Eric, though thou'lt not believe me.

*Eric.* No, no.

*Osr.*            'Tis true, howe'er thou think it strange :

Go, ask my liegemen, if thou doubt my lips,

Who have fought with me, and confess'd me lord,

Since first young Osric slipp'd his leading-strings.

But see, the sun hath seized on yonder wall ;

Support me to the window : 'tis most sweet

To look on nature at this budding time.

Sweet breath of spring, how thou renewest me !

    *Eric.* Here you may have a fair and distant view.

    *Osr.* The rosy morn, upon the hills uprous'd,

Brushes the dewy lawn with flying feet,

Descending to the plain : the dappled clouds

Course o'er the flow'ry fields ; the light bee hums

In the shy bosom of the blushing rose.

Hark, Eric, how the lark his matin sings,

Far risen in you deep blue crystalline ;

His chorus, all creation, full and strong.

The hounds are forth upon the distant hills,

With eager bay rousing the noble chase ;

The horn winds through the dell ; the forest glades

Ring gaily with the whistling woodman's stroke ;

The ploughman's smack is heard, and hearty voice,

Urging his oxen through the cloddy fields ;

And see, reflected in the sleeping lake,

The snowy breast of yon proud-sailing cloud,

That o'er its mirror stoops, and hovers there,

To gaze on its own virgin majesty.

Sweet scene of beauty !   O perfection sole !

O bright reflection of celestial things !

How calm and gracious is thine influence,

How deep, and beyond utterance, thy pow'r !

Methinks, my veins swell with the tide of youth,

And that I am no more a weak old man,

The while I gaze on beauty.   Oh, she hath

A sov'reign spell to lift the weary soul

From this dark maze, wherein we, lost, do pine,

To happy mansions of immortal bliss,

Where only freedom dwells and true content.

Let him be envied of all grosser men,

Whose heart, not hooded o'er by worldliness,

Can truly feel this precious influence,

For he alone can know felicity.

'Tis an elixir of perpetual youth,

That, e'en beneath gray hairs, can save for us

The happy thrill of childhood, and beguile,

By repetition of familiar sights,

Our souls to the glad times when we were young.

Dost know, my Eric, I sometimes inquire,

Within myself, when on these scenes I gaze,

If all my middle life were not a dream.

I have breathed peace so long, that warlike thoughts

Seem but the memory of another world,

And marvel how this wither'd arm I lift,

Once grasped Lord Osric's sword, the fiery Dane,

Who tore this castle from its Saxon lord.

I am transported to my youth again,

By gazing on these old familiar sights,

By giving ear to these remembered sounds :

Thus sang the merry lark when I was young,

Thus joyfully would bark the nimble hounds ;

The breeze thus whisper'd, mid the summer leaves,

His amorous-complaining melody ;

And thus in youth the brook flow'd silverly.

   *Eric.* What, is Lord Osric old ?   Not so ; old age

We measure not by counting of our years,

Nor by the snows bedrizzled on our heads,

But by the infirm soul.    Could you but hear

The trump of war!    Ah! there's Lord Osric's vein.

    *Osr.* Eric, thou'rt old to be a flatterer.

    *Eric.* 'Tis but your modesty that calls me so,

For uttering an universal truth.

    *Osr.* There was a thing that troubled me last night;

'T has slipp'd my memory.

    *Eric.*                Why, this it was:

My lady Ethelburga stay'd from home;

'Twas nightfall, and a storm raged o'er the wood,

Was terrible to see.

    *Osr.*          When came she back?

    *Eric.* Ere midnight, safe.    To tell a foolish tale,

That should be chidden on an old man's tongue;—

The storm, for shame to have so rudely beat

Upon so fair a creature in his wrath,

To show his dumb contrition to the maid,

On either cheek had hung a wat'ry pearl,

As speaking-precious as an angel's tear.

*Osr.* What escort had she with her?   Didst thou see?

*Eric.* An armèd company : 'twas so, in truth.

*Osr.* Why so?

*Eric.*          In happy time here comes your squire :
Sir Esmund will inform you of those things.


*Enter* ESMUND, *in haste.*


*Esm.* Good morrow to your lordship.   Here's a morn
To bring fresh roses into wither'd cheeks :
By Heav'n ! it fills my soul with luxury :
As balmy, thrilling, and restorative,
To those who feel their current on the ebb,
As that fair Shunnamite, whose sweet young breath
Fann'd David's cheek, as on his breast she lay.
You've risen early.

*Osr.*          Esmund, what's thy news ?
Not peaceful, for I see thine armour's on :
And such a forc'd smile plays upon thy brow,
As when the sun strikes through embattled clouds.
Smile all, or be all frowns ; be peace or war.

And why dost thou approach so hastily ?

I am no soldier, if some mischief lurks not

Under so hot a tread.

    *Esm.*               Regard it not,

My lord.—This message, Eric, to the men.—

                              [*Exit* ERIC.

And yet in truth I could have wish'd I had

A tale more fit for venerable ears.

    *Osr.* Away, this shy beginning of rough things !

This soft and maidenlike exordium,

That ushers in the flaming majesty

Of glorious war !  Forgett'st thou who I am ?

Osric, am I, a soldier, and a Dane.

How dar'st thou preface to me I am old,

When thy next word's of war ?  I know it, I.

What ! think'st thou I've no strength ?—Within there,

    Eric !

Bring me my weapon from the armoury.—

I'll show thee in a trice, what I can do.

    *Esm.* Oh, sir, content you for a little space.

*Osr.* I've slept too long of late ; I own 't, with shame :

In peace, a soldier grows luxurious :

But 'twas occasion for mine arms that slept,

And not my need, that wink'd on exigence.

Peruse my person o'er : are these the limbs,

That usually accompany old age ?

'Tis luxury that drains the strength of man,

And rots him ere the timely stroke of death.

In the first fire of impetuous youth,

And when my weightier arm proclaim'd me man,

'Twas still my glory to be first afield :

With all my soul I did attend upon

The shrill-sped summons of ennobling war ;

Yea, my heart hung upon it, as its food :

And now I'm old, shall I forget myself ?

Then Osric were not Osric, but his tomb,

And lives to chronicle a man that's dead.

I tell thee, Esmund, when I hear that note,

By day, or stretch'd upon my bed at night,

If but one limb can to the other move,

Or stand at all, old Osric shalt thou see
Helm his gray hairs to do a martial deed,
Arm his scarr'd breast, and to the battle ride,
Through banded shields to pierce to his brave sire,
Who from the blessed halls of Odin show'rs
Sweet looks upon brave deeds.

*Esm.*                               Had I been told,
Or had I dream'd there lay so fresh a soul
Under that white and wrinkled bark of life,
I still had doubted it.    Oh, I want words
To meet this marvel !    To the saints be praise,
That have prolong'd your vigour with your days.
Your valour shall have speedy breath, my lord.
I hope, I've not offended.

*Osr.*                    Oh, no, no !
Esmund, I love thee well ; I know thee for
An honest and a right brave gentleman.
But, prythee, keep me in suspense no more.

*Esm.* Thus rumour doth report : a Saxon lord
Hath lately with a troop possessed the forest ;

'Tis said, moreover, that he claims your castle.

This hearing, I (oh, pardon it) concealed ;

Partly, for rumour is a liar approved,

But chiefly, that I fear'd t' imperil you,

Being old, with such fierce news ; though I was wrong
      there :

But truth spoke out last night ; for as my lady,

Guarded by me, pass'd homeward in the dusk,

Some men sprang from an ambush suddenly,

And seized your daughter.   On the instant, I

Drew, and defended her ; but being press'd

By many weapons, and my lady in act

To be borne off, and knowing that a troop

Was station'd near, I ran with all my strength,

And brought them in ; at whose approach, the men

Fled for their lives, and left your daughter harmless.

   *Osr.* Now by my sword, if I have closed mine
      eyes

That robbers may o'erleap the pales of law,

And ravish in the face of open day,—

What, 'neath the very frown of this my castle !—

I am unworthy to have lived so long.

*Esm.* My reputation to a jester's bell,

If these were robbers !   O my lord, not so :

I know what kind of creature is a thief ;

Pale, stealthy, timorous, brave but by night,

Slinking, like ghosts, from day : but these were men,

Whose faces were as open title-deeds

Writ to all present and to future times,

By nature's hand sealed with her ruddiest blood

Unto possession of this fair round earth,

And for a name, term'd Saxons.   See, my lord ;

Here comes one to confirm me.


*Enter* OSWITH.

*Osw.*                      To Lord Osric,

Mine embassy.

*Osr.*          Lord Osric hears you, herald.

Say first, who sent you.

*Osw.*                  From Lord Edwin, I

5

Bear this demand ; either restore this castle,

Now my Lord Edwin's, by inheritance

From his deceased sire, Lord Ethelwulf :

And whereof he, the said Lord Ethelwulf,

Was formerly disseized by violence ;

Or, failing this condition, name a day

Whereon, supported by what pow'r you have,

You may oppose Lord Edwin in the field,

And, to award of the just God of battles,

Submit your title ; which to be conceived

In the set teeth of justice, law and honour,

My master now avers, and, trusting to

That high imperial Pow'r who ever arms

Right with His majesty, sends you, by me,

Defiance, with this glove.

　　*Osr.*　　　　　　　　A moment, stay.

I ask thee, herald, is thy lord a knight ?

　　*Osw.* By the hand of Richard, Duke of Normandy.

　　*Osr.* Why then, Sir Esmund, take the challenge up ;

And, gentle herald, bear this answer back :

Since, without God inspire, our actions all

Are weak and nerveless as an infant's arm,

Nay, wither'd ere conceived in our will's womb,

So by His aid did I obtain this castle,

And so by His continuing grace will I

Retain 't ; so let thy lord consider well

How he array himself against a man

So prosperous and well with God as me.

But if thy master, in contempt of life,

Would spit himself into the jaws of death,

And drag his comrades after (whose sad state

Moves me to tears), Lord Osric's wont is not

To baulk a foe in the pursuit of glory.

When honour calls him, and his fame's at stake,

A man must loose the bonds of charity,

And from his bosom thrust each kindly thought

To wither in the fiery sun of war ;

Till, in the eve of the contention's heat,

His foe upon the green cool turf doth lie,

And to compassion of a brave man fall'n,

Unseals the parch'd fount of the victor's tears.

Tell him, in fine,

Lord Osric, on the seventh day, will dare

His utmost valour upon Brackley moor.

*Osw.* Nobly deliver'd ! As the bird of Jove

Gives warning of a king, so flying Fame,

That through all Christian countries spoke of you,

Advised us of a brave and courteous knight.

Accept my thanks, and with th' assurance you

Find in your breast, credit Lord Edwin too.

*Osr.* This chain of gold was once a Swedish knight's,

Whom on the plains of Germany I slew.

Ah, rest his soul ! he was a gallant man ;

His fellow lives not now. Wear't for me, sir.

*Osw.* I thank your lordship, and so take my leave.

*Osr.* Farewell, sir, and commend me to your lord.

[*Exit* OSWITH.

I never heard a man more dignify

Himself in speech. If but the oracle

Shame not his mouthpiece, this young Saxon lord

Were worthier to live Lord Osric's friend

Than perish by his sword.   Spirit of battles,

Thou true Promethean spark, how thou rekindlest

Cold nature in my limbs !   But now, I was

As one benumbed with winter, reft of soul,

Heavy and sapless as a fallen tree ;

Now my blood dances like a spring-touch'd brook.

I think, life hath her seasons circling round,

And youth comes in upon the rear of age.—

O God ! I thank thee, that Thou hast vouchsafed

Some glory still to my far-travell'd sun,

Ere it decline to its dark western tomb.—

What ! rouse thee, Esmund : is thy joy so mute ?

Oh, then, thou'lt weep upon thy wedding day.

Why hang'st thou thy sad head so leadenly ?

And bit'st thy lip ?   Man of my heart, what ails

      thee ?

Art thou translated into Osric's body ?

Thou hast a look of age.

    *Esm.*           And reason for it :

When Wisdom is by old men thrust away,

Fain must she dwell with youths.

   *Osr.*                      I see, thine eye

Labours with meaning.   O' my faith, I'll 'scape thee :

I'll not be midwife to so wise a babe.

Thou art too prudent to be merry, sir,

When merriment's becoming.   I'll at once

Go forth, and marshal all my warriors.—

Nay, speak, man, if thou wilt ; discharge that look.

   *Esm.* My lord, my lord, could words to weapons turn,

Or valour in one breast rout a whole army,

Against all men, yours were the victory.

But oh, bethink you of your humble means

To follow these proud thoughts.   Alas ! how slowly

Performance limps after our wingèd wills.

Your men are few in number, lazy, proud,

Gross-bodied, feeble, mut'nous to the core,

And from the bloody clasp of war long free,

Are fall'n asunder through lax discipline.

Horses, and arms, and warlike furniture

Are more defective than you can suppose.

Ah, my dear master, that I should say this!

But when your heart finds this brave utterance,

Mine own refuses to respond Amen.

    *Osr.* Now, for mine honour's sake, I must reprove thee.

Had I not proved thee by experience

To be beyond suspicion a brave man,

I'd tell thee to thy face, " There spoke a coward."

What man who lives, or from his grave can boast

That e'er he took Lord Osric at surprise ?

Hast thou not heard me tell of the Lord Stein ?

    *Esm.* Alas! my lord.

    *Osr.*               I think thou dost forget.

In Denmark, on a time, my castle stood

Perch'd on the swart brow of a pine-clad rock ;

And the Redhand (for so they call'd Lord Stein)

In the still hours came suddenly upon me.

Jesu ! was war within the skies that night :

The wind did battle with the chimney-stalks,

Hurling them from the roof ; the gaunt trees roar'd,

And toss'd their mighty branches to and fro,

Contending in their strength ; near and more near

The iron step of Thor roll'd o'er the hills,

Shaking the vault of heav'n ; and, in the midst,

Fearfully quench'd, the lamp of night went out,

And darkness swallow'd up both earth and sky.

But from the casement of my castle-keep

As through the gloom I gazed, a single flash

Tore the obscurity ; was something moved,

And glitter'd in the light ; I knew 'twas arms :

I rous'd my men ; in silence deep we arm'd,

And secret watch'd behind the close-barr'd gates.

Softly our foes came climbing up the steep,

From crag to crag ; full eighty men in steel :

But when now half was gather'd at the edge,

We drew the bolt, and with a cry rush'd forth.

Then o'er the thunder rose the din of war ;

Shout answer'd shout, and arms rang horribly :

The screams of falling men appall'd the night,

Remorselessly hurl'd o'er the steep incline.

Flamed o'er with a pine-torch, the Redhand stood ;

He raised his battle-axe, and rush'd at me :

Sweyn took the blow upon his lifted targe,

And, flashing round, my great two-handed sword

Descended on his shoulder ; low he fell :

Then turn'd his men, and, leaping down the rock,

Fled cow'ring o'er the plain, their recreant backs

Turn'd to the pale eye of the tim'rous moon.—

We bore him swiftly through the castle gates,

Unarm'd him tenderly, and laid him down

On mine own couch.   Alas ! thrice gallant foe,

Wast then, alas ! wast then a dying man,

Though all the glories of Walhalla shone

In thy bright hero's eyes.   Softly my hand

Thou took'st in thine, and with a sigh that bore

Thy spirit on its wings, thus murmur'd forth :

" Thy castle, my Lord Osric,

" Is like a thunder-cloud, wherein Jove sits,

" That, being but reach'd at by ambitious hand,

" Doth shoot forth instant death."   His eyes grew dim,

And his brave spirit was in happiness.—

O Esmund, in those days were men indeed !

But for these shallow youths of Saxony,—

The very spawn of these degen'rate times,—

'Tis but to don our steel-coats and ride forth,

Or, like the famous Greek, great Peleus' son,

Peep o'er the battlements and shout at them,

And further they'll not stay.

*Esm.*                     Oh, that a man

By too much courage should undo himself,

And by assurance arm his enemy !

Oh, rouse thee, gallant lord ; shake off this dream :

Time runneth on the while your thoughts sleep fast.

Prosperity is in the hand of Heav'n,

And earthly fortunes are as shifting sand.

*Osr.* Hath anything befallen to my men ?

Why, think ; 'twas but the other day I storm'd

This castle with a regiment of fire.

*Esm.* Pardon, my lord ; 'twas twenty years now since ;

And of your men most part are in their graves :

Some few still linger in the eye of Death,

Who, like a gaoler, in their footsteps walks,

Stealing his shadow o'er them ere himself :

Pale, feeble, toothless, sunken in their cheeks,

Some blind, some deaf, some wanting of a limb,

And scarce a soul but drivels in his talk :

E'en as the last few wither'd leaves of Autumn,

Left to bewail their too long living hap,

While Winter, stern and pale, comes frowning in ;

Grey ghosts of strength, mere memories of men,

Stray gleanings from the busy hand of Fate.

   *Osr.* Was it so long ?   Oh, let me pause awhile.

But wilt thou tell me it was twenty years ?

Yet let me think :—Oh, yes, oh, yes ! it was :

O memory ! O Osric ! fallen ! fallen !

Vain-glorious man, what dost thou meditate ?

Thou quench'd light, wilt thou be flaming still,

And glitter in the front of warriors ?

Osric, thou hast grown old : thine hairs are grey ;

Thy brain hath turn'd to folly.

*Esm.*                              Give me leave——

*Osr.* Nay, Esmund, I have done with flattery.

Whom sorrow teaches, learns his lesson well.

Those sweet delusions of old age have fled,

And cleared mine eyes, that now I see these limbs

Are wither'd, halt, and feeble.

*Esm.*                              I but thought

To check you flying madly, not to bring

That lofty and thrice noble spirit to earth,

Pierc'd with so sharp a pang.   Do I not love you?

*Osr.* I know thou dost, my Esmund, and I turn

To thee more confidently in that thought.

Listen : my life hath met with some applause ;

I have reaped glory with a sweating brow,

And fame so earned is sweet, sweeter than life.

Should this young Saxon come upon me now,

When I am feeble and enthrall'd by age,

Fast bound in sickness and infirmities,

And, pilf'ring from me mine illustrious name,

Leave me defenceless to the cruel tongue

That stings misfortune to the quick! O Esmund,

In one disgrace, ingloriously slain,

Should Osric and his honour lie entombed.

*Esm.* Far, far, my noble master, be such end

To such a life.

*Osr.* Look, Esmund, on thy youth

I lean the burden of my fourscore years :

Staff up mine ancient honour, lest it fall,

And bear me to my grave.

*Esm.* And so I will ;

And, with His aid, who fights for a just cause,

Will bring you honourably through this strife.

Yet longs my heart to utter a request.

*Osr.* What Osric and his honour can accord,

Be sure is thine.

*Esm.* Oh, let me be forgiv'n,

If in this hour I shall presume too far

Upon my vantage. You, my lord, have oft,

When I improved your men in martial arts,

Both praised my skill and heaped me up with thanks

For its unbought bestowal.  Many years

Have I served you with many services,

Nor asked reward.  When danger threaten'd you,

Mine eyes have wearied out the starry night,

To watch the coming of your enemies ;

And oft (for now I dare confess so much)

That your grey head might know tranquillity,

And nightly on a quiet pillow lie,

Have I, unknown, join'd battle with your foes,

Fought secretly, and without glory conquer'd.

  *Osr.*  For which I could desire myself more rich

Of recompence.

  *Esm.*  And I myself more rich

A thousand thousand times in services

To merit that I ask ; which, if you grant,

Both beggars me of claim and runs before

To make my future bankrupt.  Ah, my lord !

Seeing that all men serve for recompence,

And without motive, none, for what serve I ?

What object have I set before mine eyes,

Whose wishèd consummation nerves my limbs

To labour in the painful race of life ?

Thyself dost know (who trulier than thou ?)

What witchery beams from the eye of Fame,

Who, in the vision of all noble spirits,

Stands vested in a thousand heav'nly hues.

Some desire knowledge ; 'tis a godlike thirst ;

And earthlier spirits burrow still for gold.

But me, thou seest, by nor fame nor wealth

Enthrall'd, nor the request of learning sweet :

The prize is still to find, that lures me on.

What fancy sprung of earth or air seek I ?

Oh, scorn me not, because I answer, love ;

Ah ! fame and wealth are shadows to pursue ;

For who can clasp them to his beating heart,

And rest content ?   But 'tis not so with love ;

That hath a form and beauty palpable,

To gaze upon, touch, circle, and enjoy,

Till drownèd bliss wake in Elysium,

And turn to his celestial food again.

Who seeketh fame, must walk companionless;

But sweet society attends on love.

Wisdom still treads upon a precipice,

And oft with thought grown giddy and brainsick,

Down topples into moody discontent:

But he who loves, and is in turn beloved,

Lock'd up and bosom'd in his own content,

Looks from the shelter of a happy heart,

And with unenvious eye sees Folly throned,

And robed in honours proudly bear herself;

In sweet and inward contemplation wrapt

Above the thoughts of sad mortality.

Ah me! what gold, digg'd from the depths of hell,

Shall be compared with Love's golden locks?

What glory, harp'd upon strange lips, outweigh

The sweet report writ in Love's beaming eye?

In presence of the king, what fool were he

Should court the lent light of the minister!

E'en so the man, who woos Philosophy,

Nor first does homage at the shrine of Love,

Who oft the risen soul hurls from his seat,

And bends his proud neck to entreat a child.

But when adorèd Love dwells in a man,

And sways the fury of his warring thoughts,

Oh, then, his fancy, from brute sense refined,

On viewless wings cleaving the liquid sky,

Can soar beyond the eagle in her flight,

And pass the swallow that wings o'er the sea.

Yea, oft such vigour is in mortal man,

When through his chaste eye Love on beauty looks,

From thought to thought, from bliss to bliss led on

Through a succession of bright images,

Into the imperishable sea he breaks,

To visions in immortal glory bathed,

Where Justice, Temperance, and Virtue dwell,

Hymning sweet music to the ear of Heav'n:

So spake the holiest man of ancient Greece,

Wise Socrates, upon whose shoulder sate

Apollo, in the likeness of a dove,

And whisper'd oracles into his ear.

Ah me ! to laud so sweet a sovereign

I have a mint of phrases in my brain ;

But the swift feet of all-too-nimble Time

Fast follow on my breathless fluency

And bid me thus to sum mine argument,—

That he who wealth desires or earthly fame,

Seeks but a shadow, a mere gilded name ;

But he who after Love his footsteps bends,

He travels on the road in bliss that ends.

    *Osr.* Assuredly some god possesses thee ;

'Tis not thyself who speaks, but he through thee.

But name to me the lady of thy heart.

    *Esm.* My lord, she is your daughter, Ethelburga.

    *Osr.* Ha ! this proves me more blind than I am halt,

Else surely had mine eyes discern'd so far.

Alas ! I fear thy suit's impossible.

Why, man, she is a marriage for a king :

I have had offers—Oh, she is the star,

The polar star, of gazing noblemen,

By whom his heart's affections each doth steer.

Full many an honour'd knight—ay, that he has—

Hath sought her hand, and for her favour swore

To rid the world of Turks, yea, to perplex

Hell with slain heretics ; but, being old,

I could not bring myself to part from her,

That she should vanish from me utterly.

 *Esm.* Heav'n knows, as I would have you think, my

  lord,

I never thought to prosper in this suit.

Fortune hath not so smiled upon my life,

That my heart's hopes are swell'd with insolence ;

But as a sick man tells to all the world

The tedious story of his sufferings,

Without respect of who can cure his pain,

E'en so my sorrows did out-talk my hopes,

That, heavy with despair, still droop'd behind.

And yet I would those words were still to say,

Which have put separation 'twixt us two.

Now forth I go, to wander through the world,

And seek for comfort where no comfort is.

Farewell, my lord ; henceforth account me dead ;

For so I am, my light of life being fled.

   *Osr.* Why, look, I did not bid thee to despair :

Jesu ! how swift of thought these lovers are !

Esmund, were I to grant thy wishes now,

When I am old and hardly borne upon,

Some men might say I chose my interest

Rather than Esmund for my son-in-law :

And yet I swear to thee it is not so.

Though many men my daughter have desired,

Of all her suitors I esteem thee most,

And willingly would make her o'er to thee.

   *Esm.* My gracious lord ! what thanks have I for
     this ?

   *Osr.* But stay, first must I question her desires ;

For I so nicely weigh her happiness,

That if she but thy little finger hate,

Or take exception to a hair of thee,

No further mention must be of this match.

I will go presently, and talk with her.       [*Exit.*

*Esm.* Ay, go to her, and my soul go with thee,

To teach persuasion to thine aged lips.

The sire look from thine eyes, speak in thy tones,

And touch her bosom with authority!

Oh, may thy silver hairs and cruel needs

Move her to pity!   There are some would say

" 'Twere satisfaction small to lover's fire

To wed a wife that she might love her sire ;"

But such ne'er loved; for who that does can look

Beyond possession of the thing he loves?

There thought, being quench'd in its own too much

    bliss,

Travels no further in futurity.

But if this hazard prove unlucky too,

Then to Lord Edwin I myself will hire,

And, with my soul, purchase my soul's desire.    [*Exit.*

## SCENE III.—BEFORE THE CASTLE GATES.

*Enter* EDWIN, *disguised as an aged Dane.*

*Edw.* Ye stately tow'rs, ye proud-eyed battlements,

Under whose bending brows suspicion shrinks,

And wraps him closer in his counterfeit!

Oh, yet again, I greet ye : hold ye still

Young Edwin in remembrance ?   I am he,

Though sadder by some twenty years than when

Ye saw my childhood.   Ah, debauch'd of Fortune !

Time-serving traitors, flatt'rers, summer-friends !

And could ye from a stranger ward the winds,

While he who own'd ye, loved ye, to the storm

Gave his unshelter'd head ?

Yet soft ; my love doth sanctify your guilt :

Guilt ! 'tis mine own, for branding ye with it,

Being usurp'd so sweetly : lightlier fold

My lady in your kind embracing guard

Than the close portals of the willing rose

The soft intrusion of the pretty bee.

While Edwin toss'd upon the weary deep,

Here cradled was his love, that is his soul ;

Then may 't be said, he never roved at all :

How love can varnish o'er a bitter thought !—

But time slips by the meditative man,

That should be seiz'd to purpose. Here's the horn

That parleys with this castle : at this blast

Fly Fortune to my aid. [*Winds the horn.*

*Enter* HOSKOLD.

*Hos.* Old man, what want you,

That thus you boldly dare the echoes wake ?

*Edw.* Rest, and a morsel, sir, for Jesus' sake.

Look, I am old, and I have travell'd far :

The palsy 's in my limbs ; see, how they shake :

My spirit faints for lack of nourishment.

*Hos.* Beggar, away ! and to a convent hie ;

Here's no besotted den of monkery.

*Edw.* A surly soul behind so fair a face !

Sweet beauty sourly marr'd is man's disgrace :

If thou wilt nature's favours not supplant,

Look not so darkly on a suppliant.

I prythee, let me in.

  *Hos.*      Begone, thou cheat ;

The flatt'ring tongue proclaims its own deceit.

My fingers 'gin to twine about my staff :

The hound hath smelt thee out ; hark, how he growls.

  *Edw.* Thou wilt not let him tear me ?

  *Hos.*         Yes, I will.

  *Edw.* I will amaze thee with some wondrous arts,

Which from the cunning Saracen I learn'd.

Such virtue can I breathe into a sword,

It shall cut stone ; but mace, nor battle-axe,

Swift-flying arrow, nor steel-headed lance,

Shall aught avail against thy coat of mail,

When I have charm'd it.

  *Hos.*     Let me see thy hand.

Fellow, where didst thou get that jewell'd ring ?

Thief, thou hast stolen it : give it to me.

*Edw.* What, scoundrel, what! dar'st thou call me a

thief?

I'll break thy head, to mend thy manners, boor.

[*Strikes him.*

*Hos.* Help! murder! within there!


*Enter several Retainers.*

1*st Ret.* Has the knave fled,

Who made thee roar so lustily to us?

*Hos.* The ancient hypocrite has three men's strength.

2*nd Ret.* Let see, if he be man or miracle:—

Come, snow-bedeck'd volcano, to thy staff.—

This is the prettiest match that e'er I saw.

A ring! a ring! stand round.

*Hos.* Ye are all fools:

Ye know, I fear him not.

2*nd Ret.* The ancient man

Hath still a nose to smell a coward out,

For all his looks of Jove, and big round voice.

A ring! a ring! Th' old man shall have fair play.

*1st Ret.* Be silent: see, Lord Osric comes this way.

*Enter* OSRIC.

*Osr.* Peace, hounds! Unruly curs, who gave ye leave
To bark down order by my castle gates ?
Off, to your work! Begone, ye idle knaves.—

[*Exeunt Retainers.*

Old man, why com'st thou here, to stir up strife
Among my people ?

*Edw.* Hear me, my good lord.
I did but crave your servant for some food,
To be repaid with labour of these hands,
(For yet I am not altogether weak,)
And with the account of some amazing arts
Practised in foreign countries, wherein I
Boast skill ; when he, this late prostrated rascal,
Branded me thief, which so unfroze my age,
I was a youth again.

*Osr.* Inhospitable boor, out of my sight! [*To* HOSKOLD.

Shall my repute be dimm'd for such as thee?

God knows how long, but yet the day's to come,

When to the wretched Osric bars his doors.—

Go, get thee in, old man; supply thy wants. [*Walks aside.*

*Hos.* This be the plaister to my smarting skull!

[*Aside.*

That mine eyes flash'd not to a soul that's dull:

Me with a feather my least babe subdue

Till I cry quarter, if this be not true;

No old man knock'd me then.   The sun hath shone

On many a disguise before this one.

I'll to Sir Esmund, ere it be too late,

And show him Saxon written on my pate.        [*Exit.*

*Osr.* Aid me, ye heav'nly pow'rs! give me not o'er

[*Aside.*

To ruin in mine age: with sweat and blood

Mine honours were acquired; let not another

Reap the ripe harvest of my painful youth.

*Edw.* This ancient man should be mine enemy: [*Aside.*

I thought him not so old.   Time ne'er look'd on

A braver record : though his strength be fall'n,

The soul of dignity, o'erspreading him,

Makes ruin glorious.   How with manliness

Is sweetness intertwined !   In his eyes glows

The setting majesty of world-wide honour.

An angry cloud mars his serenity ;

Something has ruffled him.

 *Osr.*      She loves him not, [*Aside.*

Or so she hinted ; further I'd not press her,

Lest my necessities should woo her, not

Her inclinations.   God !  'tis pitiful

That the estate and honours of a man,

The scant reward of toil and many wounds,

Should in his weak old age be reft from him

For a girl's whim.   My fate's at Esmund's call ;

If he desert me at this pinch, I fall.

Heav'n's will be done !   Old man, why stay'st thou here ?

          [*To* EDWIN.

Go, get thee in.   Ha !  tarry : didst thou not

E'en now, upon a sudden spur of ire,

Level that swaggerer ?

*Edw.*  He soiled mine honour :

Foul-spoken knave, vituperative cur !

I would his lesson were to teach again ;

Under your pardon always, good my lord.

*Osr.*  Thou'rt wither'd, lame, old, seeming impotent :

Where gott'st thou strength for the puissant deed ?

*Edw.*  In honesty, my lord, and th' unquench'd fire

Of soul, that tamely ne'er put up with wrong.

This, the reserve on which an old man draws,

In the decay of sinews and brute flesh.—

Have I your pardon for it ?

*Osr.*                Oh ! fear not :

I thought not to reprove thee ; rather thou

Deserv'st esteem.—Oh ! I am moved by this ;

And it hath turn'd the tide of sorrow back,

Wherein my manhood lay a-perishing.

If slight occasion and a trifling cause

Can rouse such virtue in a beggar's limbs,

Heavy and stiff with age, whose soul, belike,

Ne'er knew the honourable exercise

Of one high thought by which t' inspire anew

The wither'd sepulchre of mortal strength—

Being fretted to the shadow of a shadow

By care and poverty, shall Osric whine,

When peril looks at him, because he's old ?

Crave aid because his hands are sinewless ?

And bend his proud knee to his own esquire,

For lack of other recompence ?   Oh, wake!

Awake, thou soul of Osric, and cast off

This chain of years, which doth environ thee.

Forget, ye limbs, that Time, the cormorant,

Hath prey'd upon your rounded manliness.

Ye fingers, ye must learn again to fight.

Brighten, ye aged eyes, with one last gleam,

And then be quench'd in honour.   Hark, old man ;

                                        [*To* EDWIN.

How say'st thou ; wilt thou stay and serve with me ?

   *Edw.* Full weary am I of my wandering :

My feet are sore with tracing countries far ;

So is my heart most sad and desolate

With measuring the vast unbounded sea :

Here gladly would I rest my feeble age

From the long sorrows of my pilgrimage.

    *Osr.* Doubt not thy welcome.    For thy first employ,

Go, seek the knave on whom thy rousèd hand

Scored salutation, and require of him

Mine armour, which bring hither.    I am fixed

                  [*Exit* EDWIN.

Not to ask aid I cannot recompense :

The love I bear to my true-thoughted squire,

Makes me to wish my daughter had as much.

Alas ! what tongue, though the sweet Attic bee

Flew from his thymy bow'r in the blest shades,

Or though Apollo spake, or lofty Jove,

Might, to her plain advantage, urge a woman ?

Yet, when the wooing's maddest to be heard,

Though priest and parent hang upon her gown

With weight of all their reasonable saws,

Her heart is lighter to be borne away

Than vagrant straws upon a gusty day.

But Heav'n so framed them, doubtless, with advice.

To force them to discretion, 'gainst their bent,

As ruffian fathers do (whom God requite!),

Were as to build in sand, steer the wild wind,

Or on the ocean force stability.

God's blessing with her! she shall please herself.

Brave Esmund hath my pity : I must meet

His sickness with employment.   At the court

Of Norman Richard stands my cousin high,

Count Robert ; to his care I will commend him.

O holy Odin! can this be my armour ?

       [*Enter* EDWIN *with armour*,

Come, rusty mirror, let me look on thee ;

Show Osric his chang'd self.

 *Edw.*     It has lain by

For years.

 *Osr.* For full fifteen.   Come, lace my greaves :—

Nay, 'tis too tight ; ah ! tenderly, I pray.

Soh ! now my mail ; give 't to me in my
hand.

*Edw.* Let me support you, or you will not stand.

*Osr.* Is this the sword, O Osric, thou didst wield,

And like Jove's angel flash'd o'er Saxon hosts ?—

Support me to you seat ; I'll rest awhile.    [*To* EDWIN.

How happy wert thou in thy low estate,

Fellow, didst thou but know 't !   Within thy face

A lecture's writ, that makes the reader sad :

Alas ! how oft have I remark'd thine eye,

Wherein thy soul did manifestly sit,

Scan o'er these walls, ah ! feast upon the stones,

Till envy with a sigh raised from thy depths

Brimm'd o'er thy cheek in brine.   I marvel much

How such a sordid and earth-bound desire

Inhabits still so reverend a man.

Couldst thou experience the cares of wealth !

The painful bridling of licentious youth,

The ceaseless toil of still-pursuing manhood,

And then the terrors of infirm old age

To be despoiled in his feebleness

Of all the winnings of his lustier years ;

Then haply wouldst thou bless thy poverty

That sings in presence of the highway thief.—

My helm ! Pull 't off, pull 't off ; I cannot breathe.

   *Edw.* Some water, within there ! my lord is faint.


      *Enter* ETHELBURGA, *with retainers.*

   *Eth.* O saints and angels, what a sight is this !

The water ! give 't to me. Keep back ; ye press

Too close about your lord ; give him more air.—

Sweet life, lift from thy bosom thy dear head,

And ope thine eyes again.

   *Osr.*              Ah, Ethelburga !

   *Eth.* What evil, subtle, and designing man

(My worst ill wishes tend upon him still !)

Possess'd thee to affront those limbs, which nought

But reverence should clothe and soft attire,

With such a martial dress ?

   *Osr.*           Nay, prithee, cease :

Child, art thou mocking me, that art thyself

Cause of this exhibition of my folly?

*Eth.* What now you mean, I know not.

*Osr.*                                  Ay, thou'rt kind ;

So wilt be to thy life's end : when I drop

Into my grave, though thou hast help'd me there,

Thou'lt kindly cover me.   'Tis in the voice

And manner of some women, this deceit ;

But hath no more of kindred with their grain

Than the rose colour on their cheeks.

*Eth.*                                  My father,

Tell me, in what have I offended you.

*Osr.* Nay, but in nought, my sweet and gentle girl ;

Forgive me, for my wits are wandering.

Know'st thou, a Saxon chief hath challenged me ?

*Eth.* No, not till now : what reputation has he ?

*Osr.* 'Tis young lord Edwin, son of Ethelwulf,

From whom I took this castle.

*Eth.*                       Why delays

Sir Esmund from his duty ?   But to speak

Of war was once to arm him ; e'en so swift

His sword flew to his thigh, his helm was on.

'Tis not his custom to be so remiss.

 *Osr.* O Cupid ! is the story still to tell ?

Girl, girl, where are thine eyes ? Alas ! he chose

Thy silly self for his divinity ;

And thou disdain'st him in the usual way

Of worshipp'd maidens.

  *Eth.*    He has left you then.

 *Osr.* Why, wouldst thou have him languish in thine

  eye ?

 *Eth.* And therefore you are arm'd, and these poor limbs

Are lock'd in bitter steel ?

 *Osr.*    No more of this.

Sweet Ethel, to thy chamber.

 *Eth.*    Oh, that e'er

So weak and trivial a thing as I

Should sever two such spirits, one my sire,

The other not being less than noble Esmund !

Forgive me, sir, for I am much to blame ;

Yet pardon me, because I am a maid,

Whose privilege it is to be twice wooed.

Let him desire me in my humbler mood,

And I'll be changed.

*Osr.*                Thou heart without compare !

Angel of mine, my dearest Ethelburga ;

Not while my lips have any breath at all !

What, pretty fool, would'st thou deceive thy father,

These silent martyrs in thy face the while ?

*Eth.* How, sir?

*Osr.*            Thine eyes are witnesses against thee

Of violence intended to thy heart,

Which therefore in her windows sets these tears,

Like melancholy peeping prisoners,

To tell the world of cruel wrongs within.

*Eth.* You are mistaken.

*Osr.*              Nay, not I, my child :

Think'st thou to 'scape a father's watchful eye ?

But come, cease weeping, and shine forth on me :

Unfreeze my frosty vigour with thy smile.

Ah ! thou'lt dissolve me, if I linger more.

Go, sweet, and in thy chamber cloister thee

From the rude clamours of shrill-sounding war.

Thy pure soul, having privilege of heav'n,

Thither I'll send thee, my ambassador,

To beg a ghostly legion to my aid.—

Old man, I had o'erlook'd thee ; thou seem'st feeble.

[To Edwin.

*Edw.*   I'll   be   your   henchman,   porter,   scullion,
   groom ;

Hew wood, draw water ; let me sweep your halls,

Only to live with you.

*Osr.*                   Fear not for that ;

I love thee, for the love thou show'st to me.

But be not vex'd, if I require thee not

To follow me afield : thou seest my daughter ;

Thy present service is to tend on her :

I charge thee, love her heartily.

*Edw.*                   My soul

Be forfeit, if I do not.

*Osr.*                    Then farewell.—

Come, soldiers all, attend me to the field.

[*Exeunt* OSRIC *and retainers.*

*Eth.* Let me read o'er the volume of my heart :

[*Aside.*

Now on the first leaf is Sir Esmund writ :

Ah ! many a virtue is summ'd in his name ;

His valour, prudence, skill, shine forth in gold :

He loves me too ;—oh ! but he loves me deeply ;

Am I a woman, and not answer that ?

*Edw.* Hear me, sweet lady.

*Eth.*                    Can I see my sire,  [*Aside.*

To whom my life is all in duty owed,

So brave, so feeble, so necessitous,

His white locks so with glory shone upon,

Totter all ruinously, and know that I

From 'twixt his fingers have pluck'd forth the staff

On which his life leant ?   Shame, to stay so long !

I'll close my heart's book and peruse no further,

Content to wed Sir Esmund.

*Edw.*                    Madam, hear me.

*Eth.* Begone, begone, thou troublest me.—I'll read

[*Aside.*

No further in my heart, lest I meet that

Shall start me from my purpose, and cast loose

Me miserable.   Ah, this love! this love!

That, like a cross wind in my soul uprising,

Blows ope the second page.   Who was this stranger?

Go to, false framing lips, to call him strange

Who dwells in my heart's heart!   What word was

    that!

Yet whosoe'er he was, one thing is plain,

That duty for his sake seems like a Gorgon;

Turns me to very stone to think upon it.

But, O dear youth, I do devoutly pray,

Thou hast not done my heart that injury

To lightly speak thy love.

*Edw.*                  No, on my soul!

*Eth.* How know'st thou that?

*Edw.*                    I am his friend.

*Eth.*                                    Whose, then ?

Didst thou o'erhear me ?   Man, how dar'st thou come,

And creep into my secret counsels thus ?

Begone, thou rev'rend subtlety !—His friend ?

But art thou now in very truth his friend ?

   *Edw.* Ay, madam, I might say we were one flesh.

   *Eth.* Tell me some news of him ; but first, his

       name :

Is he not noble ?   As men speak, I mean ;

For that nobility which nature makes,

His patent 's on his brow.

   *Edw.*                          And dost thou love him ?

   *Eth.* My heart were void of joy, could I say no ;

Yet to my sorrow must I answer, yea.

   *Edw.* These sorrows, that do usher in sweet love,

Are like the clouds and wat'ry mists that hang

Upon the bright cheek of a summer morn :

But when the hours bring forth the blessed Sun,

Through all this weeping, sad, funereal host

He darts the splendour of his midday beam,

As enemies to his glad sov'reign state;

Which soon being melted and dispersed to nought,

Then all goes happy, fair, and tranquilly.

*Eth.* At least, I thank thee for thy prophecy.

But thou delay'st to give me news of him

Whose sight shall gild my sorrow.

*Edw.*                    First, thine hand:

He hath no older friend than I myself;

This kiss is for his sake.

*Eth.*                Hark! some one comes.

Step hither with me, and say what thou know'st.


*Enter* ESMUND *and* HOSKOLD.

*Hos.* Look, yonder stands the man of whom I spoke:

See, how securely the bold traitor smiles,

Engaging with my lady: look you now,

He takes her hand.

*Esm.*            'Tis strange, she lets him do it.

*Hos.* Kisses it, by St. Peter!

*Esm.*                So he does;

And she, whom I accounted Virtue's self

(For so she is to me), chides him as one

Who rather chid the manner than the fault,

Because 'twas not committed on her lips.—

Go, fetch a guard.—That fellow told me right :

[*Exit* HOSKOLD.

'Tis like, this man is the young Saxon chief.

Soul of my fathers ! can it be he loves her ?

But what imports that now he's in my pow'r ?

Transparent youth, how he shines through 's disguise !

Can eighty years tread o'er the earth so light ?

To hands press lips of fire, with murmurs breathed

Upon the burning wings of deep-drawn sighs ?—


*Enter* HOSKOLD *and retainers.*

Release my lady's hand, thou counterfeit !

But for her presence, I would strike thee dead.

   *Eth.*  Sir Esmund, I'll not stay to quarrel with
      thee.

This ancient man had from my father charge

To tend on me : see, thou oppose him not.

Come with me to my chamber, good old man.     [*Exit.*

 *Esm.* Stay yet awhile.     [*To* EDWIN.

 *Edw.*        Why wilt thou hinder me ?

 *Esm.* To tell thee that I know thee for a spy.—

Arrest him, fellows : 'tis the Saxon chief.

 *Edw.* Am I discover'd ?   God and my lady, then !

 *Esm.* Lord Edwin, thou but runn'st upon thy death :

Yield up thy sword to me, and thou shalt live.

 *Edw.* To fight such odds were folly; here's my sword:

Heav'n and mine own just cause fight for me now !

 *Esm.* Go, fellows, bear him quickly to a cell ;

On peril of your lives if he escape.

     [*Exeunt retainers with* EDWIN.

Upon his finger shines a jewell'd ring ;     [*To* HOSKOLD.

Possess it while he sleeps, and bring it me.

     [*Exit* HOSKOLD.

Since honourable means have fail'd their end,

I will seek out this chief's bereaved men :

They, doubting not the voucher of this ring,

Will gladly to his rescue follow me :

Thus shall I win the castle.   But meanwhile

With certain desp'rate rovers will I treat

To ship Lord Edwin o'er the distant seas.

Most like his men (as sheep left shepherdless

Betake them to the wolf for government)

Will choose myself to be their general.

Thus shall this castle and its gem be mine :

Upon the guilty deed kind fortune shine !                    [*Exit.*

# ACT III.

## SCENE I.—THE FOREST.

*Enter* HUBERT, OSWITH, THEODORE, *and others.*

*Hub.* Nay, sit thee down: why, boy; why, merry
romp,

What's come to thee ?   A song, sweet child! a song !

*The.* No ; I'll not sing.

*Hub.*                        But if thou knew how I
Am musically bent this afternoon !

*The.* 'Tis not your wont; for when I sing to you
My prettiest airs, you talk, or make a noise,
Or move away, while I am singing best.

*Hub.* Oh, then I was not so inclined as now :
All pleasures have their season ; those we most

Affect, not being desired at present time,

Fall coldly on our spirits : who can brook

A merry tale, being busy, sick, or sad ?

Dainties delight us not when we are full ;

So sweetest sounds fall flat upon our ears,

That chime not with the passions of our souls :

But now mine inmost spirit is athirst

To drain the pleasures of sweet harmony.

*The.* I do not care for that ; I will not sing.

*Osw.* Will you not sit by me, boy ?    Watch me now ;

I'm making arrows of the yew-tree wood :

See, how I shape them smooth and taperly ;

Head them with steel, and feather them so swift,

They'll overtake an eagle.

*The.*                    'Tis all one :

I've seen you do 't before.

*Osw.*                    Not with this knife :

This pretty knife is quite unknown to thee.

*The.* I'll look at that : who made it ?

*Osw.*                         I myself

Carved out the handle from a huge stag's horn :

The blade was temper'd by old Thor, our smith :

The handle's wrinkled like cook Frigga's face ;

The blade is sharper than her nose.

*The.*                              Ha ! ha !

I love you when you say such funny things.

*Osw.* Why, sit thee down, and eat thy supper then.

*The.* No ; now I've seen the knife, I'll run away :

Maybe, Lord Edwin will return to night :

I'll climb the hill once more, and look for him.    [*Exit.*

*Osw.* What ho, lad, stay !

*Hub.*                              Thou'dst better let him

    run.

Since my Lord Edwin to the castle went,

A prowling spirit has possessed the lad :

He is as restless as a little bird

That's wander'd from its nest : he will not eat ;

But frets about the forest all the day ;

While sorrow is so gather'd in his eyes,

Needs but another drop to swell it o'er.

*Osw.* He's right; 'tis strange, Lord Edwin comes not
back.

*Hub.* I greatly fear, some mischief has befall'n.

Hark! some one comes this way :—Ho! who goes
there ?

*Enter* ESMUND.

*Esm.* A friend of the Lord Edwin's.

*Hub.*                                   Oh, most welcome !
What news bring you of him ?

*Esm.*                                Art thou the man
Who, in his absence bears authority ?

*Enter* THEODORE.

*The.* Just now one came this way.  Oh! there he
stands :                                               [*Aside.*

His back 's to me ; but now he turns himself.

O holy mother ! 'tis the wicked squire :

That villain has dealt fouly with my lord ;

But if he's still alive, I'll seek him out.          [*Exit.*

8

*Esm.* I have a message to you from your lord;

But, doubtless, first you'd hear some news of him.

*Osw.* Ay, that's the main; first tell us, how he fares.

*Esm.* Unlucky are the lips that teach the crimes

Of Fortune wreak'd on spirits of great worth.

Would that another man of sterner mould,

Whose heart choked not the passage of sad truth

Might paint my dearest friend in misery!

Briefly, the worst; your lord in prison lies.

Ye know, beneath what weight of aged snows

Your lord had cover'd up his youthful fire;

And how his honour and proud chivalry

Lay hidden in the base weeds of a Dane:

E'en thus he enter'd in Lord Osric's castle,

Who, like a courteous knight and gentleman,

Shot forth kind welcome on his suppliant.

By chance a knave was idling in the hall,

A shrewd, suspicious, snarling, saucy knave,

Who, coming near Lord Edwin viewed him close;

Till, spying on his finger this rich ring,

With lifted voice, *Ho, ho, thou knave!* cries he,   ·

*Is this the badge of thy great poverty?*

*Where got'st it, thief?*   Whereat Lord Edwin's soul,

Through his poor habit flashing, gave him forth.

   *Hub.*  O, who, by putting on a sordid dress,

Can hide the spark of proud nobility ?

What garb can Brutus teach to play the slave ?

Ah, my dear master ! it has come to this

Because thou sett'st at naught old Hubert's love,

Calling him "preacher" with thy fiery lip

For moving thee to quit this rash design :

Oh, thou hast slain thyself!

   *Esm.*             Forthwith Lord Osric

Bade seize him, who resisted not, where no

Resistance had availed ; and so he was

Cast fetter'd into prison.

   *Osw.*             Tell us, sir,

How came you to befriend him ?

   *Esm.*             Thither I,

Proceeding secretly, conferr'd with him.

He, of my love being satisfied (it sprung

From certain jars betwixt my lord and me),

We thus compounded ;—To Lord Edwin's men,

Making but threat of arms, my influence

Should ope the castle gates, and (life apart,

Which to be spared) his should be all the spoil :

Upon which consummation, he should yield me

Lord Osric's daughter, to become my bride :

These terms consider'd, he consented to,

And wing'd me with this message hitherward,

Adding this ring for further testimony ;—

Look at it; 'tis your lord's.

  *Hub.*     I know it well.

You have but to command, and we'll obey.

  *Esm.* Why then, by all the love ye bear your lord,

And by the oath that ye have sworn to him,

Who now in darkness lies and fetters sharp,

Hung o'er, alas ! by cruel threat of death ;

Betake ye to your weapons, seize your bows,

Swords, battle-axes, pikes, or what ye have,

And set yourselves in my obedience,

For we'll attack the castle instantly.

*Hub.* Oswith, go thou that way, and sound thy horn :

I, on this side, will call our comrades to.—

In half an hour we will be all met here.        *Exeunt.*

———◆———

## SCENE II.—A PRISON.

*Enter* EDWIN.

*Edw.* If, to have come within the reach of joy,

To have talk'd familiarly and sweetly with it,

Have held it by the hand, and kissed it too,

Can, by comparison, arm present grief

With pang more keen and bitter to be borne,

Then am I truly to be pitied.

I had esteem'd myself more of a man

Than to be so moved by adversity :

I have forewarn'd my breast of troubles oft ;

Proposed griefs to my fancy ; taught my heart .

To anticipate the loss of what it loved,

As friends, life, liberty ; and thought by this,

Being so admonish'd, when misfortune came,

'Twould find me adamant : but now I see

The seeming steel of this philosophy

Pierc'd by the rude thrust of an accident ;

And myself, naked of all comfort, left

To the bleak pelting of the pitiless storm :

For, with what forethought we encase ourselves,

There's still some chink unthought on ; through the which

Misfortune creeps, and the defence is lost :

Nor can our sum of miseries be cast

Until experienc'd home, more just than he,

Who, standing on the comfortable shore,

Can tremble with the tossing mariner.

I have lived not unhappily ; yet deemed,

At any time, I could have look'd on death

With an indiff'rent, dry, and sated eye,

Nor held the grave more fearful than my bed,

Until one day made life a blessed thing,

And the next brought my doom.    O God! O God!

Thus to be snatch'd away so suddenly,

When life was fairest, and Hope at her noon

Made of this usual earth a festival

And paradise of sweets, where'er I turn'd !

E'en in the sunny hour of maiden love,

And when my heart, swoll'n high with too much bliss,

O'erflow'd this common world of things, that all

I touch'd, or tasted, heard or look'd upon,

Seem'd fraught with a new pleasure !    O, 'twas hard !—

But to my pray'rs again !    I have sinn'd much ;

Yet haply He, who judg'd me, may repent,

As once He did for erring David's sake :

Though let me, for my safety, take good heed,

I mock Him not with service of my lips.


*Enter two Rovers.*

Who's there ?    What are ye, who thus darkly break

Upon my meditations ?

1*st* *Rover*.           Hist, no noise !

Speeches are cutthroats : not a word, sir thane !

We come to take you hence.

 *Edw*.                    Ha ! whither would ye ?

 1*st* *Rov*. You'll know more certainly when you are

  there.

 *Edw*. I will not go with ye until I know.

 1*st* *Rov*. Pinchcheek, thou hast the cord ; go, bind

  the lord.

 2*nd* *Rov*. Is he a lord ?   The devil from his eye

Hangs a most ugly sign.

 1*st* *Rov*.           Pinchcheek, thou'rt sober :

I will report thee sober to our chief.

Where is thy valour, sir ?

 2*nd* *Rov*.           Thou hadst it last.

 1*st* *Rov*. In verity, here 'tis, in my left pocket.

Drink !  drink !

 2*nd* *Rov*.      Now, thane ; I fear thee not, not I :

Here goes to bind thee, thane.

 *Edw*.                    My death's resolv'd on ;

And, by the God I serve ! I will die here :

I will not budge an inch.

    2nd Rov.           He will not budge.

    1st Rov.  Pinchcheck, another dram ! this time for

    wisdom,

Because thou giv'st despair so little line.

The thane talks nature : who can root his feet

With willing heart out of his native land ?

Haply our children, climbing on our knee,

Have found the windows of our bosoms ope,

And, pretty fools ! crept in, and nestled there.

Or else our sad wife, standing on the shore,

With kerchief at her dim o'erflowing eye,

Weeping and waving at moist intervals,

Is like a sight of death to look upon.

Or else we leave a maid, our sweet first love,

Our own peculiar and heart-doting treasure ;

With many a kiss sealing her constancy,

And oaths to double-lock her plighted troth,

So sail we forth upon the boundless sea ;

Beyond the blue horizon stretch we on :

But when we come again, when we return,

I say, when we come back :—what talked I of ?

Pinchcheck, the thread !

> *2nd Rov.*              The cord ? here 'tis.

> *1st Rov.*                                    Fool ! fool !
> I ask'd thee for the thread of my discourse.

> *Edw.* Thou foolish drunken fellow, what's thy name ?

> *1st Rov.* Drawcork, an 't please you, sir: was butler
>    once
> To a monast'ry, and learn'd my letters there.
> O, I can talk :—Pinchcheck, be evidence.

> *2nd Rov.* Yea, thou'rt the opiate of the elements ;
> I've seen the stormy wave, when thou harang'st,
> Hang down his crested head, o'ercome with sleep,
> And low'r it on his placid heaving bosom.

> *Edw.* Away ! out of my cell ! ye trouble me.

> *1st Rov.* Why then, come quietly.

> *Edw.*                            I will not go.

> *1st Rov.* O, what a sweet simplicity is this,

When mortals kick at sheer necessity!

Thou, to that arm, Pinchcheek; I'll carry this.

   *Edw.* Let him attempt me, who's in love with death.

Weak knaves, ye weary me! out! get ye gone!

[*Driving them out.*

   1*st Rov.* Run, Pinchcheek, to the shore, and bring

      more aid.                  [*Exeunt rovers.*

   *Edw.* And yet, I do repent me to have fought

So hard against the swift sure hand of Fate.

Am I a Hercules to laugh at armies?

Or god, akin to the dire elements,

That, single-handed, thus I dare my foes.

'Tis said, the anticipation of an ill

Is th' ill itself; nor has death any pang

But what we make ourselves by thinking on it:

Ay, could we lift our thoughts beyond this life,

And hold for nought the idols of our hearts!

So, as I am a Christian, let me do it,

And purge my heart of earth:—farewell for ever,

Thou sweet delusion; thou dear vanity!

Thou momentary dream so fraught with bliss,

That, hov'ring but upon the verge of slumber,

Scarce show'd thyself most fair, and thou wast fled !

Fair flow'r of earthly hope, born but to die,

Fall'n on a soil so all unfortunate !        [*A lute outside.*

Is this an angel, come to sing my dirge ?

 *The.* (*sings outside*)—

   A pilgrim stood within the hall,
    And spake this trembling word,—
   "O Lady Margaret, I bring
    Some tidings from thy lord."

   "And is he well ? " in haste she cried ;
    "O wilt thou never speak ? "—
   "Ay, well ; though many a tale of woe
    Is writ upon his cheek."

   "And shall I soon behold my lord ? "
    Her breath she quickly drew ;
   For, from within the stranger's hood
    A stifled sob came through.

   She gazed : he turn'd the hood : she saw
    Lord Stephen's noble crest ;
   And swoon'd, and without motion lay
    Upon her warrior's breast.

*Edw.* It is my Theodore, my prettiest Greek !

O thou disposer of all good, hast thou,

To warn me of thy near advancing grace,

Sent on thy smallest angel from the sky ?—

Hist, Theodore !—Sweet boy, he cannot hear me ;

The casement is so small, and set so high.

O, for some means, to teach him where I am !

See, here's a tile that's fallen from the roof ;

My dagger's point shall be my pen for once :-

" *Between the castle and the neighb'ring shore*

" *Post, with all speed, a dozen men at arms.*"—

My heart with thee, thou speechless messenger !

Thou bear'st Lord Edwin's fortunes in thy flight.-

The boy has pick'd it up ; he waves his hand,

And kisses it to me :—run for thy life,

Thou pretty ling'ring fool !—I think he hears me ;

So swiftly o'er the ground his light feet fly.

Hark ! I hear steps along the corridor :

I will do what I may to draw out time.

SCENE III.—A ROOM IN THE CASTLE.

*Enter* OSRIC *and* ERIC.

*Osr.* Tell o'er thy news again ; my soul abjures it :
Esmund, a traitor !

*Eric.*               Ay, within this hour
The scouts predict him here.   Bear up, my lord ;
You take this news too heavily.

*Osr.*                    O Esmund !
I loved thee, Esmund ! rear'd my hopes on thee,
Leaned my infirmities upon thine arm,
Trusted thee with mine honour.   Let the staff
Henceforth cast off its owner, and the ground
Under the superstructure yawn its grave.
Ungrateful man ! thou eat'st at mine own table ;
What secret of my heart held I from thee ?
Or what possession thou might'st not have shared,
So near my bosom ?   I am an old man ;
And my last words must be, all men are liars.

Heav'n pardon thee for this, thou cruel man,

To have deceived me so !

 *Eric.*      We should not grieve

As though no man had suffer'd pain before ;

Or think, because we grieve, our fates draw on

Some solitary special-pointed curse.

Sorrow is such true link 'twixt man and man,

That oft we comfort and much solace draw,

By the remembrance of another's woe.

How many noble spirits, ere your own,

Pierc'd by the sharp point of ingratitude,   `

Have felt how deeply those they love can sting.

 *Osr.* Go, go ; I cannot reason with my grief ;

Could I but do so, I'd no grief at all.

When I'm in pain, what comfort is 't to think,

That Cæsar suffer'd too ?   What's he to me ?

Each heart 's a sep'rate world ; and feels no more

Another's grief than parallels can meet :

To think on Cæsar's pain, soothes me as much

As Cæsar consolation drew from mine.

*Eric.* Well, here comes comfort of another kind ;

And so I'll leave you, to collect some news.      [*Exit.*

*Enter* ETHELBURGA.

*Osr.* O my supreme of cares ! God shield thee, child,

With stouter arm than mine !

*Eth.*                    You call'd me, sir :

What would you with me ? but the tale that has

So drear a frontispiece, must needs be sad.

*Osr.* Ay, Ethelburga, thou must read with me

The book of sorrow.   Ah ! my gentle girl,

When I did teach thee first thine alphabet,

How testy and how wayward didst thou seem,

Fighting at each step of my patient love :

How oft the tedious book was flung away

Blotted with tears, and torn with angry fingers ;

Thyself as sulky and as full of woe

As if the griefs of Niobe were thine :

With pictures would I win thee back again

To slip instruction through thy pleasèd eye ;

And thus I wooed thee to the sweets of knowledge.

E'en such a childish and a fancied ill

Was bitter to thee, for thou wast a child ;

But now, to meet thy riper-judging eye,

Another volume is most sternly set,

Whose dark realities no art can charm,

Nor kindliest tutor to thy taste commend,—

The sorrows and mishaps of human life.

   *Eth.* Ah, sir ! give me the book ; thou'rt old to teach;

And I will be instructor in my turn :

Do thou but count thy sorrows out to me ;

And, for each sev'ral one, it shall go hard,

But I will match it with some comfort still.

   *Osr.* First, Esmund is a traitor ; fall'n away,

And leaguèd with my foes : in him all men

Seem perjur'd, for I held no man as him.

   *Eth.* Ah ! friends are still our shrewdest enemies ;

The shaft that strikes us from the hand we love,

Doth rankle in that sacred inmost part

Not all the malice of our foes can reach,

9

And wound us beyond healing.   Oh, 'tis pity
That nature, who frames heroes, yet should leave
Their tend'rest part unarm'd !   My words were boasts,
That promised comfort for an unknown ill :
Alas ! I have no balm for such a wound,
Unless it be this kiss.

  *Osr.*      The best of cures !
Bruised heart no other salve than love endures.—
But come, my angel, thou must put from thee
The woman ; in an hour the traitor's here :
Heav'n guard thee then from his polluted hand !

  *Eth.* Thou wrong'st me but to waste a fear that way.
Virtue is virtue's safeguard ; many a queen,
Wanting that last defence, in peril stands,
Though tower'd in a nation's heart of hearts
And awful with their swords.

  *Osr.*      Brave girl, 'tis pride
To have been thy father.

  *Eth.*     Is there no resource ?
What has befallen to your soldiery ?

*Osr.* My men-at-arms are rebels to the core :

Esmund did train them ; they are all his creatures.

I have experienc'd, that he, who sleeps

On his own interest, to ruin wakes.

E'en thus I found it, when I durst review

The men who call me, leader : mid the array

Mine eye did wander, and required still

Those old companions of my chivalry,

Those pillars of my heart, my noble Sweyn,

Brave Edric, and his brother Ethelward,

Knute, Harold, Leofric and Heroman ;

And finding not, whom Death had ta'en away,

But in their stead new forms and faces strange,

As chill as old Deacalion's stone-born brood,

I was enforc'd to turn aside, and weep.

    *Eth.* My comfort's dumb: but say, what happen'd then ?

    *Osr.* What then ?  Why, marry, that among these knaves,

Authority is grown a standing jest :

A chief, who, in my youth, was half a God,

Is now the whetstone for each boorish wit;

My person, arms, limbs, manner, motion, gait,

Yea, mine infirmities became their sport :

Saith one to 's neighbour, plucking him by th' arm,—

" *This is a wizard, come to fee the moon ;*"—

" *A priest by 's beard,*"—the second knave replies,

" *Where will he place him to command our march ?*"

" *Ship-fashion, at the stern,*" the fourth returns :—

Whereat being hotly moved, I drew my sword,

And smote one scoundrel to his native earth,

When instantly,—Oh, act incredible !—

As thick as startled wasps they rush'd at me,

Bound down mine arms, removed my sword away,

And mock'd mine indignation with the shout

Of my supplanter, worthless Esmund's name.

With difficulty I released myself.


*Enter* ERIC.


*Eric.* My lord, the traitor, Esmund is at hand,

With a strong force of Saxons after him :

Look not to be supported by your men,

For false as Judas is each sev'ral one.

*Osr.* Fly, Ethel, to thy chamber :—quick, my sword.

*Enter* ESMUND *and followers.*

*Esm.* Lord Osric, sheathe your weapon, and fear not ;

No thought of mine is levell'd at your life.

*Osr.* I do not thank thee for thy mercy, traitor ;

Thy thanks are rather due to these grey hairs,

If thou hast any mercy to bestow.

*Esm.* Sweet Ethelburga, I would speak with thee.

*Eth.* Too well thou know'st I cannot answer no.

*Esm.* Nay, lady, thou hast scorn'd me long enough :

Is this discreet, to frown and turn thy back,

Or, as thou dost now, through thy lifted eye

To show thy soul on fire with sparks of pride

At him whom Fortune has set o'er thy fate,

Yea, and the lives of those thou holdest dear ?

The haughty soul most suffers in the mire :

I should be sorry, to be forced to teach thee

The bitter lesson of humility.

Thou know'st, thyself hast forced me to this pass ;

Therefore do thou, without more siege of words,

Surrender, while my love's still courteous :

I could more roughly woo thee if I pleased,

Seeing thy person is my prisoner.

    *Eth.* And of my better part thou hast her scorn.

    *Esm.* Scorn is a weed that from neglect doth grow,

But love is the rich fruit of tender care.

Pray'rs are the gentle gales that quicken love,

And still 'tis nourish'd by fast-falling tears ;

Till, to the eye of the glad labourer,

Who smiles to look, it spreads its timid leaves,

And, 'neath his sunny welcome growing bold,

Doth round his bosom fast entwine itself :

Thus love is quicken'd, foster'd, cherish'd, rear'd.

So, Ethelburga, let me tend on thee ;

Since to obtain the treasure of thy love,

Shall still be all the business of my life.

    *Eth.* Eternity shall but increase my hate.

*Esm.* Then must I use a rougher argument :—

Look, Ethelburga, that thy filial hand

Pluck not my vengeance down upon thy sire !

If the fierce tyranny of the icy north

But breathe upon the solitary leaf,

Thou know'st how soon it falleth to the ground;

E'en in so frail a balance stands thy sire.

By Heav'n, I will not shrink from any lengths,

To conquer thy submission ; so reach forth

Thy hand, in witness thou wilt be my bride ;

Or else, by all divine, thou shalt bring down

Sorrows as thick as hail upon thy sire.

   *Osr.* Fellows, I will have leave.   Hear, daughter,

      hear me :

If, to the siege of that abandon'd man,

Thou but unbarr'st thy silence of a term

That hints surrender :—if thou dost, I say,

But flatter him with one beseeching look ;

A father's pray'r shall post on wings to heav'n,

And sue a curse on thee and all thy line.

*Esm.* What, am I conqueror, and bearded thus ?—

To your duty, fellows ! go ; away with him :

Go, all of ye, and leave us for awhile.—

       *[Exeunt all, save* ESMUND *and* ETHELBURGA.

Think, Ethelburga, dost thou well in this ?

What, wilt thou be thy father's murderer ?

    *Eth.* To heav'n I do commend myself and him,

E'en to that power that breaks the lion's teeth,

And from the mortal snake can pluck the sting.

In God I trust, who will deliver me,

And turn aside the aims of wicked men.—

Base man, thou hast no pow'r to injure me.

    *Esm.* Thou mak'st me mad, thou scornful girl, thou

      dost.

I am not further to be trifled with :

Look on thy lover, or Death looks on thee.

    *Eth.* Death be my choice, then, whom in sooth I love

Than guilty Esmund more.

    *Esm.*               Thyself hast put

The angel from my bosom, who till now

Hath been thy mute preserver :—enter, then,

Ye spirits of evil, and possess me quite ;

Inspire me, all ye devils ;—I am weary

Of gazing on thy beauty at arm's length :

A kiss, though it consume me !

  *Eth.*       Help, O heav'n !


    *Enter* EDWIN, *and a few followers.*

 *Edw.* Ruffian, let go !　Thou soul of treachery,

A second time hast thou deserved thy death,

And shalt thou live ?

  *Esm.*    Lord Edwin !

  *Edw.*       That's my name :

I'll set my signature upon thy heart.

 *Esm.* Art thou come hither in the flesh indeed ?

Or, but a spirit, to call me to account ?

  *Edw.* Too long a story for hot blood !—die, traitor.

  *Esm.* Lord Edwin, stay ; a moment, stay thine

    hand :

I own my life is richly forfeited ;

Yet to a dying man deny not shrift.

My soul doth wallow on the ground with guilt:

Oh, let me lighten it, ere I go hence,

And wash it with some tears of penitence.

   *Edw.* Short shrift, long cord would grace thine

      actions best.

   *Esm.* How thou cam'st hither to mine overthrow,

Against the fate I had contrived for thee,

The God of judgments knows, to pierce whose ways

Were vain.—I ask not this;—besides my time

Is all too short to urge my penitence:—

Yet can it be, I am so swiftly fall'n

Who but a moment rode so royally

Upon the proud top of iniquity?

O shame, thou art sin's shadow: e'en so close

Thou followest upon the guilty man,

Pursuing him with thine uplifted mace,

That ere the wretch hath time to say, I prosper,

Thy blow, descending on the godless boast,

Shatters his brittle greatness to the earth.

*Edw.* Continue in these thoughts, and thou'lt be wise ;
Thou hast already mended half thy fault.

*Esm.* First, shall my knee contritely sue for peace
From her to whom I did intend most wrong :—
Lady, sweet lady, pardon, if thou wilt,
The guilty aim of this wrong-seeking heart.

*Eth.* All I can pardon is remitted thee ;
And, for a free gift, thou shalt have my pray'rs,
To further thee with heav'n.

*Esm.*                          Sweet saint, how does
Thy goodness, like a fair and shining light,
Set off the depths of mine impurity !
Now could I wish to live, to learn to die.

*Edw.* Tell me, how thou wilt use thy liberty.

*Esm.* Not far from this a monastery stands,
That, from the reedy bosom of a fen
Uplifts its dark and solitary walls :
Croyland, its name ; for learning famed of old,
And od'rous memory of many a saint
Whose mortal bones enrich its sepulchres.

Thither will I, while yet the spring of life

Calls nature to rebellion in my blood ;

This martial vanity put from my side,

And all the pride and fiery lust of arms

Quench'd in the bosom of humility,

Retire with the sad burden of my guilt.

I'll change my name, that it shall be forgot,

And pass away, e'en as a leaf that's fall'n,

From the gay interchange of carnal men,

To be recorded in the book of life :

And thus, in sorrow, shall my years be told,

Till the sad tale have end.—All day, with pray'rs,

Strict meditations, and denying fasts,

Will I be instant upon Holiness ;

But when the eye of night shall gleam on me,

I will awake the fury of mine arm

To scourge the pride of this rebellious flesh,

That as a wall of sin parts me from God ;

Till mercy, peeping forth with piteous eye,

E'en from the bosom of the righteous Lamb,

Shall look upon my sincere penitence,

And drop moist quittance on my sin's account.

   *Edw.* Happy is he who so o'ercomes the world

That he can count it dross ; but few there be,

So sweetly temper'd to celestial things,

And with that heav'nly, glorious armour dight,

That they can wage this war.    Far, far beyond

All human laurels is that wondrous man,

Who, spurning the vain crowns of earth, aspires

To war against the flesh and its desires.

   *Esm.* Farewell, Lord Edwin : God hath fought for thee.

Thou hast a heav'n on earth in thy sweet bride.—

Reach forth thine hand, sweet lady, that my lips

May bid the world adieu upon 't.    Oh ! now

Farewell for ever to all earthly bliss ;

Pleasure hath passed away in this last kiss.      [*Exit.*

   *Edw.* Peace go with him, and comfort him in time !

I dare not for my conscience seek to win,

From holy mother church a proselyte :—

Forbid it, Heav'n !—but 'twas a noble mind

That should have flourish'd loftily, had not

The angry breathing of hell-heated passion

Swept o'er the buds of his ill-fated youth.—

Go, bring Lord Osric hither, some of you.


*Enter* OSRIC.

*Osr.* Young Saxon, of his own accord he greets thee ;

Thy foe, Lord Osric ; now, by fate of war,

Thy captive.   But my heart is comforted

A little, by the thought of thy brave father

Whose life I spared, and whom, with thee, his son,

I freed from bonds; more, by thy looks, wherein

Nature hath set no stamp of cruelty ;

But chiefly, by thine actions, which have saved

My girl from the lewd handling of a rebel :

All which assurances speak in me now,

When I beseech thee to restore my daughter,

That we may pass together from thy castle,

And live in virtue, if, perchance, to die

In poverty.

*Edw.*      What, am I favourite

Of Fortune to no end ?   Ah, dear my lord !

Is 't well, is 't right, to filch from victory

Its pith and kernel ?   Trust me, I'll not yield.

    *Osr.* My heart misjudg'd thee : welcome, then, the

        worst !

    *Edw.* The worst thou'rt welcome to, if thou mean this,

That I restore this castle back to thee ;

If this content thee, I've a giving mind.

I see suspicion crowd into thine eye :—

What, ho, my men ! attend to what I say :

Into Lord Osric's hands, I, with this ring,

Consign your duty and obedience.

    *All.* Lord Osric ! we desire no better chief.

    *Osr.* What means this riddle ?

    *Edw.*                              But for this choice part

Of Fortune's favour ; even for her who makes

All riches cheap ; this gift will I retain,

And with my life defend it.

    *Osr.*                        Dost thou love her ?—

What say'st thou, Ethelburga?   Mute?   Yet so

Looks not a maid when she would answer no.

    *Edw.* What, not a word?   Oh, then thou lov'st me

        not.—

Am I a child again, that will not read

The characters my very soul doth know?

O ecstasy, that dims mine eyes, to trace

All Cupid's volume writ in one sweet look!

    *Osr.* When I was young, I too could read that book.


        *Enter* THEODORE.

    *The.* A prodigy, my lord! a prodigy!

    *Edw.* What, Theodore? come hither, bird, to me:

Sure, heav'n ne'er pack'd an angel closer!   How

Shall I reward thee?   Oh, no way but this,

My love shall wipe the debt out with a kiss.

    *The.* O, hadst thou seen his sides all white with

        foam,

His parch'd tongue lolling from his gory mouth,

That dewed the ground; so stiff, so feeble too!

So meek with sorrows and so gaunt with years,

Withal so gentle !   Yet I weep for him ;

For he is dead : oh, would he were not dead !

*Edw.* Why, silly child, what art thou telling me ?

Wilt thou persuade me thou hast seen a ghost ?

*The.* Hubert and I stood by the castle gates,

And look'd toward the forest.   Twilight grey

Under her mantle dark had stol'n the trees

To sleep with nature, while all sounds reposed ;

When, from his covert in some secret glade,

Advancing feebly o'er the misty plain,

An aged wolf crept slowly into form.

Stiffly he paced, for he was old and gaunt ;

Yet proudly, as he were the forest's lord :

At times, pent sighs burst from his shaggy sides ;

And in his eye, methought were human tears,

So thick the drops coursed down his hairy cheeks ;

While oft he bent his muzzle to the ground,

And snuff'd the dubious scent : but when he came

Within an arrow of the castle gates,

He stood stock still, and mutely look'd to us.

With wonder moved at such a prodigy,

Together shouting at the beast we ran,

And thought to scare ; but lo ! the brute stood still :

We struck him hard, and still the beast stood stock ;

Only upon me he upturn'd an eye

So meek, so pitiful, so wobegone,

That round his hairy neck I flung my arm.

Then onward to the castle gates he moved,

Though now for weariness his head hung low,

While many a foamy flake bedew'd the ground ;

Till, being come within the gate, one set

A little water to the animal ;

Which wistfully he eyed, and dipped his tongue ;

Then stretch'd himself upon the earth full length,

And with a gasp expired.

 *Edw.*    Is here a man

Skill'd in divining ?   If there be, let him

Come forth, and say what means this prodigy.

 *Eric.* Now is my time to speak, lest heav'nly signs

Shine to the eyeless.—Look on me, Lord Edwin !

Canst thou not recognize these lineaments ?

   *Edw.* Eric, my father's henchman !

   *Eric.*                           Even so.

My life has been prolong'd to see this hour,

That I may be the interpreter of Heav'n.

The wolf is guardian of your noble house ;

For ages in this castle has he couch'd,

Fed by the hands of your famed ancestors ;

But from the shadow of those evil days,

Back to the woods he fled, and ne'er was seen,

Until the sunshine of this blessed hour.

Oh, truly, in this pregnant happy sign,

Heav'n's voice doth whisper in no parable

The gracious promise of her bounteous truce ;

Therefore, be happy, lord, for thou hast leave :

Only be virtuous, lest thou offend.

   *Edw.* O thou who look'st o'er all, shine in me now,

And teach my heart to sing its gratitude !

   *Osr.* Well bears he fortune who thus pays his thanks.

*Edw.* The noble wolf is in his halls again ;

The log doth crackle on his ancient hearth ;

With ruddy welcome smile the hoary walls

Upon Lord Edwin, and upon his bride.

Spread forth the board, and let the cup be raised

With ruby flowing to the crystal brim :

Shout, hearts ; be merry, all ; the man, who's not,

Stains this white day with an unseemly blot.




THE END.

www.ingramcontent.com/pod-product-compliance
Lightning Source LLC
Chambersburg PA
CBHW021120020726
47500CB00003B/853